MOONRUNNER

Kane/Miller
BOOK PUBLISHERS

MOONRUNNER

MARK THOMASON

Kane/Miller
BOOK PUBLISHERS

First American Edition 2009
by Kane/Miller Book Publishers, Inc.
La Jolla, California

First published by Scholastic Australia Pty Limited in 2008
This edition published under license from Scholastic Australia Pty Limited.
Text copyright © Mark Thomason, 2008.
Cover copyright © Scholastic Australia, 2008.
Cover photograph copyright © istockphoto.com/Anja Hild
Cover design by Natalie Winter

Library of Congress Control Number: 2008933429

Printed and bound in China
1 2 3 4 5 6 7 8 9 10

ISBN: 978-1-935279-03-7

TO REBECCA

*Without her love and insightful heart
the beauty of this story would not exist.*

★ CHAPTER ONE ★

Running Away

"I ain't goin' back! I absolutely ain't!" No matter how hard I whipped Old Lop Ears up the dirt road, he wouldn't go faster. My throat ached from swallowing so many tears. "You dang-burned mule! Go home by yourself! I don't care! I ain't goin' back, ever!"

I yanked the reins. The mule drove his front hooves into the dirt so hard that I flew between his long ears and landed on the ground, still holding the reins. I leaped up, angry. Throwing my book bag against a gum tree, I flipped the reins over the mule's ears and slapped his flank. "Get to the shed, you dang-burned mule! Tell Ma and Pa I ain't comin' home! Not tonight. Not ever!"

I collapsed on my books, slumped against the large blue

gum tree, and fought back the tears. I longed to be back in Montana. I felt trapped in all these scrubby, spindly bushes they called trees. Montana had open spaces where I could spot a band of mustangs a mile away.

A patch of dry, rough, scrubby grass was irritating my leg so I jumped up and stomped on it until it went flat. I shouted, "I wish you were Mike's ugly face!" and flopped back down again. "I hate this place! I hate this ugly place!"

My throat felt raw, like I'd just swallowed a mountain of gravel. And that was another thing! Montana had crisp air that I could breathe. The gum trees around Omeo had paper-thin bark that looked like it was dying and leathery leaves that smelled like hair oil, and the air had a strong bitter odor that made my voice sound like a sick bullfrog. The kids at school seemed just like this dang-burned country. Ugly! Ugly! Ugly! And I hated every one of them.

Old Lop Ears was standing beside the road, head down, sleeping, waiting. The mule seemed to understand my feelings. Maybe he hated this place, too. Maybe he longed for what used to be, just like I did. Lop Ears was the only one I could tell about my sorrow and loneliness.

I removed my school lunch from my book bag, stuffed it into the saddlebag, and mounted. My books would just be in the way. I reined the mule across the bridge, but instead of turning south for home, I turned north. Near the Mitta Mitta River, I waded Lop Ears across the shallow Bingo Munjie Creek, found an easier trail, and worked my way along the banks of the larger river. I had no idea where I was going – I just knew that I wanted no one to find me, ever!

In the late afternoon, storm clouds burst open, dropping buckets of cold rain. I was getting soaking wet. Shivering violently, I tied Old Lop Ears to a dead tree limb beside a small stream that dumped into the Mitta Mitta and scrambled up a steep, rocky hill to see if I could find shelter. The way ahead along the river appeared to be blocked. Near the top of the hill I found a small overhang and curled up away from the storm.

Several hours later the rain stopped and the moon skipped out from behind the clouds. It was crystal clear. Across the Mitta Mitta, I could see jagged mountains that seemed to go on forever. Misty fog hung low between the spurs.

A flash of movement caught my eye. Instantly snapped from my misery, I spotted a mob of wild horses bursting from a hidden gully directly across the river. There were ten horses, running hard. The sound of their pounding hooves was dampened by the recent storm. From where I was hiding, I could see their wet bodies glistening in the moonlight. Two of the wild horses were spotted, like painted mustangs in Montana. The rest were solid colored, maybe black or dark red.

A black stallion suddenly appeared in the moonlight. He galloped straight towards the river. Towards me! I fell backwards, startled. He stopped and snorted loudly, challenging me to show myself. He was magnificent! My body tingled with excitement.

Prancing like a cat, with a mane and tail longer and silkier than I had ever seen, the black stallion snorted again, his nostrils flaring wildly. There was a small white diamond on his forehead beneath his black forelock. His beauty almost took my breath away. For a full minute, the wild horse sniffed the air and looked directly at me. He didn't move. I didn't move. The stallion's powerful muscles quivered as he remained perfectly still, staring at the rocks where I was carefully hidden.

As though anticipating danger, the stallion suddenly spun and followed the other horses upriver. "Moonrunner!" I whispered. "That's what I'll call you. Moonrunner." It had happened so quickly. I finally felt my heart start beating again and took a slow, deep breath. I wasn't shivering anymore. Too excited to sit still, I scrambled from beneath my shelter and worked my way down the steep incline to where I had tied Old Lop Ears.

"Lop Ears! You should've seen him – a wild stallion! I'm going to call him Moonrunner. A good name, don't you think? He knew I was watching and he just stood there! Did you see him?"

The mule stared dumbly at me. "I know ... you want to go back to your warm stall." I loosened the reins and paused, still feeling the thrill of seeing Moonrunner's glistening body across the Mitta Mitta in the moonlight. "What do you think, Lop Ears? Is it too dark to go home? Ma and Pa will be worried, I know. I shouldn't have run away ... but I don't care if Pa tans my hide good with his shavin' strop. Seeing Moonrunner was worth a thousand whippings!"

I put on my sheepskin coat that I had forgotten was tied

4

behind the saddle and started up the trail towards home. When the mule paused I glanced across the river at the bushes covering the entrance to the hidden gully.

"He's coming back, Lop Ears. Moonrunner will return at sunup. Do you want to see him again?" Duty was telling me to go home; my heart was telling me to stay.

Patting Old Lop Ears tenderly, I tied the reins around another limb near some grass and removed my school lunch from the saddlebag. "I feel guilty about not going home, but you know I have to see Moonrunner again, don't you? Anyway, Lop Ears, if you tried taking us back in the dark, you'd probably step into a wombat hole and kill us both, you silly old thing. Better to stay here. We'll get started at first light. Will that suit you? There's no wolves in Australia, so don't worry. You're too tough to eat anyway. I know you understand. I just feel like Moonrunner was trying to tell me something – something important – and I've gotta find out what it is."

I returned to the rocky cliff and did my best to get comfortable, determined to stay awake.

The thunder of hooves striking rocks startled me awake. It was dawn! My spirit soared.

I peeked over a boulder just as the small band of horses appeared. Without slowing, the mares wheeled sharply and disappeared into the brush. I strained to catch another glimpse of Moonrunner. My heart raced; my breathing all but stopped.

There he was, even more majestic in the early morning

light. Moonrunner turned and walked directly towards me. At the edge of the river he stopped, lifted his powerful head and snorted. I slowly stood to face the stallion. For a long moment we stared at each other across the river. It felt like we were the only two creatures in the whole world. The wild stallion danced proudly in the sand and challenged me to cross the river. When I didn't move, Moonrunner spun around and disappeared into the brush. I was sweating. I felt weak. I couldn't move. I was frozen in place by his challenge and his power. Again, he had tried to tell me something ... but what?

I spent the day on the rocky cliff hoping to see Moonrunner again, not wanting to go home. There was plenty of rainwater to drink, caught in little pools in the rocks, but hunger finally told me that it was time. Late afternoon had already arrived.

I heard a voice in the distance, carried on the wind. I eventually spotted a lone figure on horseback. It was Pa. I was in deep trouble! I bolted from the ledge, quickly untied Lop Ears and was doing my best to make the old mule trot when I ran into Pa riding Girlie. The relief on Pa's face made me feel guilty about running away.

"Casey, my boy!" Pa waved. "I've been lookin' all night and all day! Thank God you're alive! Are you all right, son?"

I waved and reined Old Lop Ears towards Girlie. Trying to be as casual as possible, I answered, "Sure, Pa, I'm fine. Just hungry."

"Your ma is real worried. What happened to your clothes?"

"I got caught in the rain and got a little muddy, that's all."

"It's not the mud I'm a-lookin' at, son, it's the blood. Where'd it come from? Miss Evans said you didn't get to school yesterday, or today."

"You've seen Miss Evans?"

"Course. I've been everywhere lookin'. Saw your book bag by the bridge. Thought you might've been taken by the Mitta Mitta."

"Pa, I'm sorry I've been such trouble," I answered. And I was sorry, but I was glad Pa hadn't found me last night or I wouldn't have seen Moonrunner.

"We're your family. Don't ever forget that. We stick together, you hear?"

"Yes, Pa, I know. It's just that … I'm tryin' so hard to like Australia. Wish I had a riding horse. I hate ridin' a mule to school. Everybody laughs at me. I really miss Arrowhead."

"We made a choice that was best for the family. Now, I'll hear no more about selling Arrowhead. But, since you hate riding Lop Ears, I guess you could walk," Pa answered. "Course it would take you an hour longer each way. And you'd be doin' your chores after dark. And you'd be fixin' your own breakfast, because it'd be too early for your ma to get up."

I had to laugh at Pa's logic. I played along. "Miss Evans sleeps in a room behind the schoolhouse. I could take my meals with her, make a bed under the building and come home on weekends."

"Then we'd have to rent your room to a swagman so he could do your chores," Pa smiled. "What really kept you from comin' home?" he said, smoothly changing the subject.

After a long pause, I asked, "Pa? Can you teach me to fight?"

"You been in a fight already?"

"Yeah. But it wasn't my fault. They jumped me on the way to school and laughed at me for riding Old Lop Ears. I tried to force them bad words back down their stupid throats!"

"How many jumped you?"

"Four."

"I'll have a talk with Miss Evans tomorrow."

"Don't do that! Please, Pa! I'll find some way to get even."

"Revenge ain't a good way to start a new life. Find some other way. No fightin'!"

"But Pa!"

"No fightin', I said. Is that clear?"

"Yes, Pa." I clenched my teeth again and fell silent.

"You get hurt?"

"Got a fist in the eye. My elbows are skinned pretty bad and they shoved dirt down my throat."

"What does Australian dirt taste like?"

A sudden grin split my face wide open. "It would've been better with gravy," I answered.

We crossed the Bingo Munjie Creek and turned up the trail for home. A dozen wallabies scattered into the bush and remained watching as we rode by. Too excited to keep the secret to myself, I said, "Pa! Last night I saw a mob of mustangs running in the moonlight."

"Mustangs are called brumbies in Australia."

"Brumbies? That's really weird. Worse than dunny!" I said. Pa chuckled.

"You should've seen Moonrunner! He's a black stallion. Better than any mustang I've ever seen in Montana! I spent the night on a rocky cliff so I could see him again this morning."

"Moonrunner?"

"Yeah, Pa. He was wet and running in the moonlight. The most beautiful horse in the whole world. A black stallion with a little diamond on his forehead. He was running with a bunch of mares. I waited all night. He came back this morning, like I knew he would, and just stood there lookin' at me, right across the Mitta Mitta. We're going to be friends."

"You could never make friends with a brumby like that, son. Might as well forget about Moonrunner altogether. And brumbies don't make good ridin' horses, either."

"I need a horse, Pa. There's got to be a way."

"Casey, I said I didn't want to hear any more about a ridin' horse."

"Why can't I have a riding horse in Australia?"

"Girlie pulls the bullock wagon and Old Lop Ears pulls the plow. We can't afford to feed another horse just yet. Maybe next year."

We rode silently for another half an hour along the creek. Finally, I said, "I know you're right, Pa. I'm always dreaming."

"Dreamin's part of growin'," Pa answered. After a while he asked, "You feel like goin' to school tomorrow?"

"No, but I'll go anyway."

"Stay home. Have a hot bath, let your wounds heal. School can wait."

"I'd like that, Pa."

As the sun set, when it was getting chilly, we stopped at the bridge beside the big gum tree.

"There's your book bag," said Pa.

"Yeah … still there. Books probably got wet." I slid off Lop Ears and picked up my book bag. Pa tied Girlie to Lop Ears' saddle and sat down. He leaned back against the gum tree and picked up a long stick.

"Casey? Something else is bothering you. What's wrong?"

I dropped my books and sat down beside him. The birds were quiet now. Nighttime had arrived. "Just don't fit into Australia, that's all. No one here understands me."

"What about Moonrunner?"

"Moonrunner?" A feeling of peace came over me. "Yeah, things changed last night when I saw Moonrunner," I answered.

"You mean there's hope?" When I nodded, Pa said, "You've always been a dreamer, son, so I want you to do something for me."

I sighed. I was tired, my stomach was growling and I didn't feel like a lecture. "Sure, Pa. What is it?"

"I'm asking you to reach out and grab hold of your dream, hang on tight no matter how rough it gets at school, and don't let go," Pa said. He was scratching circles in the dirt between his feet with the stick. He always did that when he was thinking heavy and about to say something serious. In the silence, he sharpened the stick with his whittling knife. At last, he said, "Your grandpa willed his homestead to us when he died. And it's a good place. It was always me and your ma's dream to homestead someplace. So after you were born we left Ohio for Montana. But I'm tellin' you now son, we hated homesteadin' that little ranch near the Wyoming border, especially in the winter when the icy wind cut through a man like he was made of paper. Your ma and me had nothin' in Montana except heartache and cold. We couldn't make a go of that place."

Pa sighed loudly. He tossed his stick into the night. I waited because I knew Pa had more to say. "Australia is our home now, Casey. This is our *new* dream. We brung Old Lop Ears and Girlie with us on the boat to make things easier. We brung your ma's rockin' chair and cookin' things to make it home. Now, let's get mounted. Food's a gettin' cold and your ma's worried."

"Australia is nothing like Montana."

"You're right. It ain't nothin' like Montana. It's much better. Unless you've forgotten, four feathered quilts weren't enough to keep you from shiverin'."

He put his arms around my shoulders as we stood. I picked up my wet books. "Son, I need your help. Ma's having a terrible time adjustin'. She's alone in this new land, too.

Nothin' to keep her company 'cept the kangaroos. Can I count on you?"

I swallowed hard. "Sure, Pa, you can count on me."

We mounted and rode towards the place Pa called home. I quietly stared into the night sky filled with strange stars.

"About them broomtails … I hear tell there's brumbies all over this area."

I looked around, wide-eyed, half expecting to see one standing across the road. "Where?"

"Back there, where you saw Moonrunner. Up there, behind the house. More wild horses here than in Montana, I hear tell."

"Can I go Saturday, Pa?"

"You got too many chores to be gallivantin' after brumbies. It may be February but winter's comin' hard. It's just like Montana. Girlie and Old Lop Ears must have enough hay cut for winter. And your ma's goin' to need help cannin' and dryin' food."

"It can't be as bad as winter in Biddle."

"You got that right. But I reckon instead of white popcorn on the Fourth of July, we're goin' to have white snow."

I really loved my Pa and the way he described things, and I felt bad about not being able to handle my own problems at school. Pa had enough problems of his own. Maybe if I tried harder …

Pa said, "As soon as the shed is full of hay, we'll both go look for brumbies. What do you think? We'll take Ma and maybe camp along the way, kinda look over our new country."

"That'd be nice, Pa." I still wasn't too happy. "Pa?"

"Yeah?"

"I'm really mixed up. I ain't never felt this way before."

"How do you feel?"

"Lonely. I miss the feel of the wind on my face when I'd gallop Arrowhead across the prairie. Even when I was alone in Montana I wasn't lonely 'cause I had Arrowhead. And I miss my baseball team. I have no friends at school. I just don't fit in down here. My best ain't good enough."

"I was in fights when I was your age. Tempers flare. Mean words are said. But listen to me son, friends will come. It just takes time, sometimes. I'll bet them boys are feelin' bad about what they done. Treat them as best you can and things'll change."

Pa looked at me, but I was still staring at the dark outline of Mount Sam. My hunger was gone. He said, "Do you remember on your last birthday? Your ma said you was lucky to reach twelve because you had a curiosity that'd kill a cat. And she was right about the curiosity. There's a light shinin' inside you that makes you very special."

"Hurtin' this much is a new feelin', Pa. I don't know how to handle it."

"It's just that you've lost your confidence for a while. Right now you're feelin' pretty low 'cause of the boys at school. But you're really growin', almost a man. You're already taller than your ma. You're skinny now, but the muscles will

13

come – especially when I let you lift all the hay into the loft. That'll help." I glanced at Pa's face and knew he was funning me. He added, "You're a downright handsome young man." His words made me feel better. "Your ma gave you her rusty-brown hair and light brown eyes. And she gave you those freckles across your nose just to remind you, every day, how much she loves you."

I smiled at Pa, but kept the real secret inside.

Three wallabies hopped across the road just in front of Girlie. "Now that's somethin' they don't have in Montana," Pa said. He finally got the mare moving again. "She's skittish. I don't think she likes Australia, either."

A silence followed. I knew that I couldn't have Ma and Pa worrying about me all the time. I had to help my parents make a go of it, especially Ma. She hadn't been doing too well. If I made things worse at school, everything would fall apart at home, too.

Before reaching the shed, I suddenly realized what Moonrunner had been trying to tell me that morning: that I wasn't alone, that he was there, waiting to be my friend. He wanted me to know and belong to his world, to be wild and free like him. It struck me that I really didn't need friends in Australia except my family and Moonrunner. I really didn't need Montana. There was a wildness in this rugged country and a wildness in those beautiful brumbies running free. Something about that wildness was just like me. There were surprises waiting for me over every spur, up every gorge and gully, hidden behind every woolly butt and snow gum. Like seeing Moonrunner across the Mitta Mitta.

Pa must have seen me staring into the night because he asked, "What's on your mind, son? Still thinkin' about them brumbies?"

"Yeah, some," I answered.

We dismounted in front of the house. Pa said, "Have your ma look at that eye. I'll put Girlie and Lop Ears in the yard for the night."

During the late evening meal, I sat quietly and only opened my mouth to pick at my food. Ma kept quiet also, which was unusual for her. Finally she broke the silence.

"You're going to have a black eye."

I toyed with my food without answering. How was I going to tell them the real cause of the fight?

"What is it, Casey?" Pa's voice cut through me like a knife. He had a way of doing that at the wrong time. When I didn't answer, he said, "Let's have the rest of the story."

I felt the words forming in my throat. I tried to force them back down into my stomach where they belonged, but they burst out.

"Was Grandpa a crook?" I saw Pa's face freeze. Why did I have to say that? I should've kept quiet. Danged me!

"What a terrible thing to say!" Ma said. "Casey! Who put that idea into your silly noggin?"

The words blurted out like vomit. "That's what everyone says at school. That Grandpa stole money to buy this place."

"And that's what caused the fight?" Pa asked.

I nodded and fought the tears dripping from my eyes. "They say that I'm like my crooked grandfather."

"Do you believe them?" Pa asked.

"I don't know what to believe!" I leaped from the table. "But I know there ain't nobody going to rub my face in the dirt again!"

I ran outside and didn't stop running until I reached the old blue gum tree beside the dry creek bed, where I fell on my face and tried to hide from the owl in the tree that was hooting at my humiliation.

★ CHAPTER TWO ★

The Baseball Game

The following morning before light, I decided to go back to school. I slipped from the house carrying a hessian bag. It's a burlap potato sack, really, but that's what it's called down here. Another weird word to remember! I placed the bag in the shed and walked around to the outhouse.

When I was little, I heard a story about a man being bitten by a rattlesnake when he was sitting in the outhouse. Ever since then, I've been frightened of going to the outhouse in the dark. It's one of my secrets. I held the lantern over the splintered opening and peered down. Seeing nothing, I placed the lantern on top of Ma's 1894 expanded Sears, Roebuck & Company catalog (her prized treasure from San Francisco) and sat down.

When I went back inside, the delicious smell of salted bacon and eggs cooking on the wood stove made me feel alive again.

Ma handed me a cup of weak coffee with sugar and milk. "That eye sure looks bad. You look like a one-eyed raccoon."

"Pain's gone," I answered. The warmth of the mug felt good on my hands as I sipped the coffee.

"Feeling better?" Ma carried breakfast over and set it on the table.

"Some," I answered. "I'm going to school this morning."

"Do you think that's a good idea?"

"Can't let them get the best of me." I sliced some bread and made a jam sandwich for my school lunch. Another piece of bread I placed on top of the stove to toast.

While we were talking Pa came in and sat down at the table, pulling up his suspenders. "I'm glad you're feelin' better, son. Figured out what you're goin' to do at school?"

"Don't worry, Pa. I ain't gonna fight no more." I turned the bread to toast the other side, dropped the toasted bread onto my plate, buttered it, and sat down to eat.

"How's that eye?" Pa asked. Ma brought Pa's coffee over and sat down for breakfast.

"Don't even notice it," I answered and quickly stuffed my mouth with food so I wouldn't have to say anything else. This morning I felt better than I had in a long while. Discovering a new hope last night had helped me decide what must be done at school. But I couldn't tell my parents 'cause they would stop me for sure.

"Come straight home from school. A lot of chores wasn't done yesterday. I'll water the fruit trees. I can't have 'em dyin' after all your grandpa's hard work."

"Sure, Pa. And I'm sorry I forgot my chores last night." I walked to the kitchen window and looked to the east. "Sun's comin' up. I gotta go. Old Lop Ears is kinda slow. Can't be late."

I grabbed my lunch and paused on the veranda just outside the door, afraid Pa was going to catch me with the hessian bag on the mule's back.

"Somethin's goin' on in that boy's mind," I overheard Pa say.

Ma answered, "Yeah, he's thinking so hard I saw the smoke coming out of his ears."

"Whatever it is, we're gonna hear about it."

I hope not, I thought. I stepped from the veranda and ran towards the shed.

———— • • ————

My eyes scanned the schoolyard as I approached the post-and-rail yard. I was the last to arrive. Unsaddling Old Lop Ears like always, I hiked towards the wooden schoolhouse with my books and lunch over one shoulder and the hessian bag awkwardly hanging over the other. A few kids gasped as I entered, shocked at my skinned face and blackened eye. The gang at the back of the room snickered, holding their hands over tight lips, trying to keep from laughing. I sat down at my desk without looking in their direction and slid the bag beneath my desk.

Miss Evans came in just after me. She was a dark-haired lady, older than Ma and Pa, and plump, with pudgy dimpled cheeks. She wore funny little round glasses balanced halfway down her nose. I really liked her.

She glanced at me, then stared tight-jawed at the boys in the back corner. She adjusted her glasses and looked back at me. "What did you bring to school, Casey?"

"Somethin' for recess," I answered.

"Well, show us."

"Yes, Ma'am," I said. Dang! Caught already. I took out my baseball bat and dropped the bag at my feet.

"What is it?" she asked.

"A baseball bat."

"What's the writing all over it?"

"My team's signatures. They gave the bat to me as a going away present."

"Why did you bring it to school?"

"Thought I'd teach a few boys how to play baseball." I placed the bat carefully across my desk and sat down, glancing only once at the gang to see if they understood my message. When they lost their smiles, I glowed inside.

Miss Evans smiled like someone who had a big secret. "That sounds like fun, Casey. Can we all play?"

"Yes, Ma'am."

"Including the girls?"

"Yes, Ma'am."

Mike called out. "Casey can play with the girls! None of

us wants to play his stupid game."

"Mike Carson! You were not asked to speak," said Miss Evans sternly. "Casey, you can teach us how to play at recess."

"I didn't bring the baseball, Ma'am."

"Well, tomorrow then. And we'll store the bat in the cupboard today. Is that all right with you?"

I squeezed my hands together without looking up. My ears burned. "Yes, Miss Evans."

"Bring it to me now."

"Yes, Ma'am."

———•◦•———

During the lunch break, I sat with my back to the largest shade tree in the schoolyard, eating my lunch alone. The gang walked by, singing.

"Sam Jenner, gobbledygook,
Casey Jenner's another crook."

I kept eating my jam sandwich, trying to ignore them. I had promised Pa I wouldn't fight. I forced a swallow. What I really wanted to do was tackle Mike and shove dirt down his throat, but I noticed Miss Evans watching from the front steps. I stood, stuffed my hands in my pockets, and walked directly towards the gang. As I forced my way through, my legs suddenly went out from beneath me. Mike had tripped me. That was exactly what I wanted. I needed an excuse to tear off Mike's head and not get into trouble with Pa. I scrambled up with a handful of dirt stuffed in my clenched

21

fist just as Miss Evans ran towards us, ringing the school bell.

The gang froze.

"Wait till tonight, Casey Jenner," whispered Mike. "The teacher won't be there to protect you. We're going to get you good."

The afternoon dragged. I couldn't concentrate on my schoolwork and I was sweating from worrying about how I was going to get away from school without fighting. A quarter of an hour before the bell, Miss Evans said, "Casey, your mule is a little slow and you've got a long way to go. Why don't you get started home?" Turning to the gang, she added, "You boys at the back, Mike, Charlie, Frank and Jimmy, the horse yard must be cleaned. My records show that it's your turn. You'll find shovels in the woodshed."

———— ·•·• ————

When I got to school the next morning, I placed the baseball on Miss Evans' desk. After our history lesson she picked it up and smiled. "We're going to take an early recess. The cupboard's not locked, Casey. You'll find the bat on the bottom shelf. It's time to play baseball."

My heart leaped into my throat. My credibility was about to be tested.

Outside, in the open area between the schoolhouse and the horse yard, eight boys and ten girls stood watching me.

"Well, Casey, let's play," Miss Evans said.

I picked up four feed bags and quickly placed one on the

ground near the schoolhouse steps. "This is home plate." I ran about fifty feet to my right and placed the second bag. "This is called first base." I placed second base in the middle of the square opposite home plate, and third base to the left of home plate, completing the square.

Returning to home plate, I picked up the bat and swung it in the air several times to relieve my nervousness.

"The object is to hit the ball with the bat and run from base to base without getting caught," I said, facing Miss Evans. "If you make it all the way around and cross home plate, your team gets one run. When the batter strikes out or gets caught, it's called an out. Three outs and the teams change sides."

"Why don't you show us, Casey?" said Miss Evans.

"Someone has to pitch the ball."

"I'll do it," Mike said. He was thirteen and several inches taller than me. Miss Evans tossed him the ball.

"You're too close," I said. "Back up. That's it. Now you need a catcher."

"I'll be the catcher," Jimmy said. "Where do I stand?"

"Behind home plate," I answered. I touched the bat to the ground and said, "About there."

"What do I do?" Jimmy asked.

"Catch the ball if I don't hit it and throw it back to Mike."

I approached home plate with the bat on my shoulder, wishing I were back in Montana playing with my friends instead trying to teach all these strange kids about baseball. Sighing, I said, "I'm ready. Pitch the ball."

Mike tossed a high-arching ball that hit the ground in front of me and bounced over the bag at my feet. "Why didn't you swing?" Mike asked.

"The ball must cross home plate between my knees and my shoulders."

"It's nothing like cricket," Mike said.

"What's cricket?" I asked.

"A better game than bloody baseball," Mike answered.

"Mike! Enough of that!" Miss Evans said.

"Sorry, Ma'am."

Mike pitched again. The ball floated across home plate right in front of me. I swung hard and connected with a thwack. The ball sailed into left field, bounced hard and rolled into the horse yard. Proud that I had hit the ball so well with everyone watching, I said, "Now, if we had been playing a real game, I'd be racing around the bases for a homerun."

Miss Evans nodded. "Well, let's play. Do you want me to choose the teams?"

"Nah, I think the boys should play the girls. Mike said I could be on the girls' team to help them out a little." The gang snickered.

The boys won the coin toss and chose to bat first. I pitched. I had Maggie, the most athletic girl, in center field so she could help the younger girls throw the ball back into the infield.

Mike was first to bat. I pitched the ball with a lot of backspin so he couldn't hit very hard. He connected anyway, hitting the ball over third base. I ran towards left field, shouting my head off, as I watched Mike run all the way around the bases and easily reach home plate before the girl in left field could pick up the ball and throw it back to me. The boys were ahead, 1–0. I felt sick inside. I desperately wanted my team to absolutely skunk the boys' team.

Charlie and Jimmy both struck out. On my second pitch to Frank, he hit a rolling ball to first base. Molly picked it up and stood there holding the ball, confused about what to do with it.

I yelled, "Step on first base!" She jumped on the bag before Frank reached it. "You're out, Frank! Good job, Molly." I signaled for the outfield to come in. "We're up to bat!" I yelled.

Gathering my team around me at home plate, I said, "Molly, you're up first. Maggie, you're second. Anna, you're third. I'll bat last. Keep your eyes on the ball and swing the bat level with the ground."

Molly hit a dribbling ball that Mike easily picked up and tossed to Frank at first base.

"One out!" Mike yelled. "Is that right, Casey? Two more to go."

Maggie stood at the plate. From the look in her eye, I could tell that she was a competitor. I was counting on her to get on base. "Choke the bat," I yelled.

She lowered the bat and turned to face me. "Why would I want to choke the bat? It's done nothing wrong."

I felt like screaming, but I held my temper. "Choke the bat means slide your hands up the end of the bat a little. Makes it easier to swing."

Maggie hit the ball. It bounced between Charlie's legs at third base and into left field. Maggie stopped at first base and jumped up and down on the bag with excitement.

I yelled, "Maggie, run to second base! George can't throw the ball that far!" She made it safely to second before the ball finally reached the infield.

When the next girl struck out, Mike yelled, "Out number two."

"I can count!" I yelled back.

He laughed.

The last of the older girls, Mary, hit the ball hard, straight at Mike. He ducked and the ball rolled safely into center field. Mary started running, but Maggie stayed on second base. Overwhelmed with frustration, I yelled, "Maggie! Run to third, run to third!" but she just stared at me, confused. Mary rounded first base and stopped on second base. Both Maggie and Mary were now standing on the same base. "Time out!" I yelled.

"What do you mean, 'time out'?" Mike asked. "What's that?"

"It means we stop the game for a minute. I can call time out if I want," I yelled back.

"That's not fair. Casey's trying to cheat us!"

I looked at Miss Evans for support. "Only one runner can be on a base at a time. Mary must go back to first base."

"That sounds fair," Miss Evans said. "Mary, go back to first base."

The next girl struck out.

"Third out!" Mike yelled. "Get into the outfield, Casey, with the rest of the girls!"

The next inning was pure frustration. Mike's team scored two more runs. He was now in front, 3-0. The game was slipping away. I suddenly hated the game of baseball. No, not hated. I just wished my own team was here. We'd show them how to play! Adding to my frustration, the younger girls struck out without hitting the ball. The embarrassment of losing my own game became overwhelming.

I struck out all three of the younger boys, but my team was still losing by three runs. It was our turn to bat, but recess was almost over. The first girl struck out. Gracie was next. She was only eight years old so I had already given up. But she approached the plate with the big bat choked and a very determined look in her dark eyes.

I watched, holding my breath. She hit the ball towards George at third base. George had been distracted by a kookaburra laughing in a nearby blue gum and the ball sailed past him.

"Run, Gracie, run! Run to first base!" I suddenly came alive as Gracie ran, carrying the enormous bat. Mike scrambled after the ball and tossed it to Frank, but Frank dropped it. Gracie was safe at first base, clutching the baseball bat against her chest like a doll, and laughing. I ran towards her, yelling with excitement. "Good hit, Gracie. I'm proud of you. Now, give me the bat."

Finally, it was my turn to bat. I hit the ball into right field. As I raced for first base, the right fielder tripped and started crying. Charlie tore after the ball, which had rolled into a dense clump of trees.

Gracie was still standing on first base. I yelled, "Gracie, run to second base!" She took off like a miniature cyclone, her dress flying, and jumped on top of second base. I arrived right behind her, almost shoving her along. "Keep running, Gracie! Keep running! Run for home plate where Jimmy's standing!"

Gracie took off across the infield for home plate. I yelled, "Gracie, no! Not that way! You've got to touch third base before going to home plate!" She reversed direction, ran around third base and crossed home plate with me right behind her.

We were only down by one run. I gathered my team into a circle. "There's only one out. We're losing and recess is almost over. Just swing easy and connect with the ball. Don't murder it!"

"How gross!" said Lucille. "First you tell us to choke the bat, and now you tell us not to murder the ball. What kind of game is this? I don't want to play anymore."

"It's only baseball words," I answered. "Please, don't you want to beat the boys?"

"Who cares?" she answered.

"Well, I do!" Maggie said strongly.

"And I think we can do it!" I said. "Who's up next?"

"I am," Molly answered.

She hit a rolling ball between first base and second base that went into right field. I ran to third base to meet her. She jumped on the base just ahead of the ball.

"Safe!" I yelled. Maggie was next at bat. I expected her to blast the ball into oblivion but she hit an easy fly ball that Mike caught with his bare hands.

There were now two outs. One more and the game would be history.

Anna swung hard and missed.

"Strike one!" Mike yelled.

I closed and opened my fists, barely breathing. As Mike pitched the ball, I held my breath. Anna connected so hard that the ball flew into left field. The fielder ran forward to catch the flying ball, but misjudged its flight. It hit the ground behind him and bounced towards the horse yard. Charlie raced after it.

Molly, who had been standing on third base, ran across home plate. The score was now tied. Anna passed first base and kept running. She was a heavy-set girl, stronger than I had guessed her to be, and a powerful runner.

I waved my arms in the air and yelled as loudly as I could. "Keep running, Anna. Keep running!"

Charlie picked up the ball. He threw it towards the catcher, but it fell short. Anna kept running. When she rounded third base, I ran beside her.

"There's time. You can make it!" I yelled. Out of the corner of my eye, I saw the ball being thrown to Mike. He quickly turned and threw it to Jimmy at home plate. Anna charged home plate as Jimmy caught the ball.

"Run over him! Run over him!" I yelled. "Make him drop the ball!"

Anna weighed about fifty pounds more than Jimmy, and was taller. I felt the thump as she slammed into him and knocked him backward. As Anna leaped on top of the bag, the ball fell to the ground.

"Safe!" I yelled. "Safe! Jimmy dropped the ball!"

"That's not fair!" Mike said, running in from the pitcher's mound. "She can't do that!"

"It's fair!" I said, jumping in front of Mike. "Jimmy was blocking home plate. Anna had the right."

Miss Evans looked at her watch. "Recess is over," she said. "Everyone go to the lavatory and wash up before returning to class. Get started on your assignments."

I was gloating. We had won! Revenge was sweet.

Mike hissed, "You had to cheat to win! Just like your grandfather. We'll get you tomorrow, cheater rat!"

I didn't know if Mike meant he would beat me in baseball or beat me up after school. But at that moment, it didn't matter. My team had won. Miss Evans walked beside me towards the schoolhouse.

"Casey, if I didn't know better, I'd swear you've been practicing with the girls," she said.

I grinned and handed her the bat. "Yes, Ma'am. This morning before school started I crept in and took the bat from the cupboard. Then, in the gully behind the schoolhouse, the girls and me practiced hittin' the ball. It was a secret, but it wasn't cheatin' was it?"

"No, that's just being smart. There's a bit of devil in you, Casey Jenner."

"Yes, Ma'am. That's what my ma says."

"How's your black eye?"

"Better now since we won the game."

"And the words are hitt*ing* and cheat*ing*, not hittin' and cheatin'."

"Yes, Ma'am."

———◆———

That night I lay awake, gazing at a half-moon through the window, too excited to sleep. I crawled across my bed and placed my elbows on the windowsill. Arrowhead used to nicker when he saw me at the window and come over to have his nose rubbed.

"I miss you, boy, I really miss you. I hope you're okay," I whispered.

Later, after the moon had disappeared, I lit a candle and held it in front of the photograph of my baseball team hanging at the foot of my bed. In the photo, I'm proudly holding my baseball bat.

"We won!" I whispered, "We won! The girls beat the

boys. Wish you'd been here to see it!" I knew that I'd never see them again, but at that moment it felt good sharing my happiness with my buddies. "They called me a crooked Yank, but I just played good baseball. And even if I lose the game tomorrow, things'll be different at school. I just know it. Maybe I can make some friends. I'd like that."

⋆ CHAPTER THREE ⋆

My Baseball Bat

They were waiting for me at the school turnoff. I was in my own world, planning another baseball game, when I heard the gang singing.

> *"Sam Jenner, gobbledygook.*
> *Cheater, rat, crook.*
> *Casey Jenner, clinkety-clank.*
> *Cheater, rat, Yank."*

All four boys stood in the middle of the road. A large bonfire burned against a boulder behind them. Mike had my baseball bat casually draped over his right shoulder.

"So, you were going to use this on us, huh, cheater Yank?" he said, swinging the bat.

I glanced around. Thick scrub was on one side of the road and boulders were on the other. No escape. I remained on the mule, determined not to get into another fight. "I ain't hurtin' you. And I didn't cheat! Miss Evans said so."

"Cheater!" Jimmy shouted.

"How'd you get my baseball bat?"

Mike just shrugged. "The same way you did when you practiced with the girls. We're going to teach you a lesson for cheating."

"Give me my bat!"

"So you don't like it here," Mike said.

I wasn't about to back down. "I like it fine. It's just you four jackasses I can't stand."

"Too bad." Mike walked to the fire, dropped my baseball bat on top and turned to see what I would do.

"That's my bat!" I jumped down from Old Lop Ears and ran towards the fire. Mike shoved me away. I shoved back. He hit a glancing blow on my nose. Pain shot across my face. Suddenly I couldn't breathe. I covered my nose to keep the blood from dripping on my school shirt. I felt someone grab me from behind and slam me to the ground. I fell hard and rolled to my back. Charlie jumped onto one arm and sat on it while Frank dropped onto the other. My legs were pinned to the ground. I mustered all my strength, yanked a leg free, and kicked Jimmy hard. He fell back and rolled away, but dived and locked his arms around my ankles.

Mike screamed, "That's my brother you just kicked!"

At least Jimmy's nose was bleeding, too. I screamed at Mike through gritted teeth, "Let me up!"

Mike's foot slammed against my head. "That'll teach you not to kick my brother!" It felt as if my ear had been split wide open. I twisted in agony, trying to break free, but Jimmy's grip was like iron. Mike piled more and more wood on top of my bat. The handle caught on fire.

I struggled to free my arms and legs. I had to save my bat. I screamed angry words at Mike's laughing face. The gang tightened their grips and held me down as more and more of the bat caught on fire. I used every muscle in my body and pushed. Charlie and Frank both fell off. Mike jumped on me and straddled my stomach. His weight forced me back to the ground. Charlie and Frank grabbed my arms again.

When I heard the school bell ring in the distance, the fight inside me wilted. I stopped resisting and just gave up. The gang stood, but I stayed on the ground in agony. I couldn't find the strength to even try to get up. I heard Mike hiss, "Go back to America, cry baby!"

The gang galloped away, laughing in triumph. I struggled to the fire, but it was too late. The handle was nothing more than burning embers. I kicked at the fire to free my bat from the flames. It spun clear and rolled across the dirt road. On my knees, I tried reading my team's autographs on the smoldering bat, but they were all blackened and unreadable.

I should've felt anger, but instead I felt grief. It was like losing my baseball buddies all over again. The bat had been a gift from my team and I'd hit a homerun with it that won our final game. It was my one connection with Montana. I was beyond tears.

I kicked what was left of the bat into the flames and sat down to watch it burn. I frantically tried to remember their faces – Johnny on first, Artie on second, Billy on third – but all I could see was the hateful faces of the gang.

When the bat was totally gone, I mounted Old Lop Ears and turned for home. Blood still dripped from my nose. My shirt was covered with blood and dirt. Ma was going to kill me! I felt very alone as the mule climbed the hill away from the school. I hunched over Pa's saddle to ease the aching in my chest. The pain in my body spread upwards towards my throat and downwards into my stomach. At the top of the small hill, where I could see Livingston Creek to the east and Bingo Munjie Creek to the west, I stopped. For a long while, I looked into the strange blue sky, gazing at Mount Sam without seeing it.

Suddenly, I screamed at the trees beside the road. I screamed at the kookaburra laughing at me. "Nothing's right here! The danged trees! The goofy birds! The stupid animals! You're all ugly! There ain't even a North Star to follow. And no one plays baseball!"

I felt like Old Lop Ears looks after plowing the field all day: beaten down, my spirit gone, not really caring what happens next. Just wanting to go home.

But where was home? Was it here in this awful land, or

back in Montana with my friends? I had been humiliated and could never face going to school again. The weight of not belonging crushed me. I sagged lower and lower in the saddle. My heart split open and deep sobs racked my body.

I wasn't aware the old mule had started down the hill towards home, stopping in the middle of the Bingo Munjie Creek bridge. There was no way I could face Ma and Pa right now. I wanted to be alone. All I wanted to do was stick my head into the ground and hide for the rest of my life. I hurt too much to run away.

Pa was irrigating our fruit trees. I could see him working with the shovel. But I wanted to be alone. I didn't need his pity. Sliding carefully down the saddle, I felt my feet touch the ground and held on until the pain went away. When I released my grip on the saddlebag, Lop Ears took off for home. I sat down, eventually scooting beneath the bridge to wash my face in the creek. That's all I could do. I eased into the deep grass, closed my eyes, and took slow sobbing breaths, trying to ease the pain in my heart.

"Casey."

I kept quiet. Maybe he wouldn't find me.

"Casey! Answer me."

"Down here, Pa."

He forced me to sit up. "Look at the blood! Anything broken?"

"Just my spirit," I answered.

"Sorry you're havin' such problems, son. I'd hoped things

would get better. For sure, I'll go to the school and talk with Miss Evans. She knows about the gang's bullyin'."

———•◦•———

A few days later, I waited alone on the steps after school for Pa to arrive for a meeting with the gang's parents. The other three fathers had already arrived and were standing together in the yard, talking. They all knew each other; we were the outsiders. Mike, Frank, Charlie and Jimmy were sitting on the split-rail fence some distance away, heads hanging, being very quiet. I was sweating like I had just finished playing a game of baseball. My head ached. I hadn't slept well last night for worrying and had crawled out my bedroom window twice to go to the outhouse because our front door squeaks.

Pa galloped in, riding Girlie, and tied her near the front of the school instead of at the yard with the other horses. I stood to greet him. "Hi, Pa. What kept you?"

He pulled my grandpa's watch from his pocket and said, "I'm right on time. Everyone else's early. Where's Miss Evans?"

"Inside," I answered.

"Well, let's go in."

The other fathers followed us inside. The gang remained sitting on the split-rail fence. At the top of the steps, one of the fathers, a big, burly man, turned and said, "You boys! Get in here!"

It looked strange for the fathers to be sitting at the

38

students' desks. I sat beside Pa. The other boys sat with their fathers, so I could tell the big man was Mr. Carson, Mike's and Jimmy's father. I felt terrible. I had caused all this. My head still ached. My eyes hurt. I wanted to disappear. I wished that I had never told Pa anything. I kept looking at my dirty boots and glancing at Mike out of the corner of my eye. He was glaring daggers at me.

Miss Evans stood at her desk. "First of all, before we start this meeting, let's introduce ourselves. I'm Miss Marion Evans. We'll start on that side of the room." She pointed at Mike's father.

"My name is Jack Carson. Mike and Jimmy are my boys."

"I'm Joseph Howard. And this is Frank, my son."

"And I'm Peter Cooper. Charlie's father."

It was Pa's turn. He stood, faced the other fathers, and pulled me to my feet. "My name's Dan Jenner. And this' Casey. We just arrived from Montana. We're farmin' the Jenner homestead across the Bingo Munjie Creek. Samuel Jenner was my father." The men looked at each other knowingly. Charlie's father held real hatred in his eyes. I looked up at Pa. He had a puzzled look on his face.

Miss Evans said, "Thank you, Mr. Jenner." She turned to face the other fathers. "We're here today to discuss your sons bullying Casey Jenner. Your sons have ganged up against him. I've seen it myself at school, so don't try denying it. If this continues, I'll have no choice but to remove all four boys from school. Casey, come up here." I stood, very slowly, and inched towards Miss Evans. "I want you fathers to look at Casey's face and split ear. Take off your shirt, Casey."

I pulled my shirt off and held it in my hand, suddenly aware of how skinny I was.

Miss Evans said, "Turn around." I turned. "The bruises are a result of Casey being kicked by your sons. And the skinned elbows are probably from Casey fighting back."

"Casey kicked me first!" Jimmy yelled.

"And when did Casey kick you?" Miss Evans asked.

"Two days ago, before school!"

"What were the circumstances?"

"Ma'am?"

"What were you doing when Casey kicked you?"

"I – we – was holding Casey down," Jimmy said.

"Why?" Miss Evans asked. When Jimmy didn't respond, she asked again, "Why were you holding Casey down?"

"'Cause Mike had built a big fire to burn Casey's baseball bat."

Mike screamed, "Shut your mouth, idiot!"

"And did you burn Casey's bat?" Miss Evans asked.

"Er …" Jimmy glanced at his big brother for support.

Mike's father leaped to his feet. "This meeting's over!"

Miss Evans slammed a book hard on her desk. "This meeting is not over until I say it's over. Please sit down, Mr. Carson." Miss Evans really shocked me. How could my teacher confront Mike's father with such strength? Miss Evans said, "Your sons are ridiculing Casey because his grandfather may or may not have cheated someone out of some money, yet I happen to know that your grandfather was a convict, sent here in a prison ship from England. This seems like the pot calling the kettle black. I think an apology is in order, sir, don't you?"

Mr. Carson's face and eyes were full of rage. "Dan, I apologize for my boys. It'll never happen again." He yanked Mike and Jimmy up and dragged them down the steps of the school. I heard him shouting, "I'm going to beat you both till your eyes bleed!"

Mr. Howard crossed the room, gripping Frank by the arm. "I'm sorry, Dan. I had no idea my son was involved in something like this. Frank, apologize to Casey right now!" Frank remained silent. "Apologize, I said!"

"I'm sorry," he mumbled.

"Why did you do it?" Pa asked.

"Mike made us," Frank answered. "I didn't want to. I liked Casey."

Charlie agreed. "Yeah, it was Mike's fault."

Miss Evans escorted everyone out of the schoolhouse. Pa and I remained on the steps of the school watching the others ride away. Miss Evans said, "I'm sorry all this happened, Casey. And I'm sorry about your baseball bat. I know how much it meant to you."

"Thank you, Ma'am." That's all the conversation I could muster. Still embarrassed, I quickly put on my shirt.

"Why didn't Peter Cooper apologize?" Pa asked.

Miss Evans shook her head, pursed her lips together and

said, "Peter Cooper wanted to buy the Jenner homestead because it's closer to Omeo than his place. And your place has water. He had it all set up with the bank. Then you arrived and presented your credentials. It's a personal thing with him."

Pa nodded. "I can deal with personal things, but I feel sorry for Jack Carson's two boys. Beatin' and punishin's no way to stop bullyin'." Pa shook hands with Miss Evans. "Thanks for your help."

"You're welcome. Casey's a fine student. A real delight." She turned to me, put both hands on my shoulders and said, "It's over, Casey. Mike's bullying you because he's jealous. He doesn't hate you. He hates himself."

"Me? Why?" I couldn't imagine Mike being jealous of anyone.

"You have a happy home life, he doesn't. You've met Mr. Carson. Imagine living with him all your life."

"It'd be terrible," I answered.

"When you see the gang at school tomorrow, be confident, be firm but courteous and walk away from trouble – but don't run. If you ever have any problems, please talk with me. But I think the bullying is over." She stepped back. "I'll see you at school tomorrow?"

I nodded and ran to the yard to fetch Old Lop Ears. Miss Evans was still standing on the steps as we crossed in front of the schoolhouse. She waved. We waved back and turned for home. Pa said, "Why didn't you tell me about your baseball bat?"

"You and Ma got enough problems of your own without

worrying about me all the time."

"It's no worry, son. Like Miss Evans said, you're a real delight. So what are you goin' to do without a baseball bat?"

"Learn to play cricket, I reckon."

★ CHAPTER FOUR ★

The Brumbies

My grandfather built our house out of rocks hauled from the dry creek and used timber beams to support the roof. The house had a large kitchen for Ma, with a cast iron wood-burning cook stove imported from England. The sitting room had a stone fireplace where Pa whittled most every night.

Grandpa chose the site because there was a year-round spring on a hill near the house. He must've been a very smart man. He built an underground cistern on the hill to capture the flowing spring water and piped our house with running water. The overflow ran down a canal to water the fruit trees beside the shed and kitchen garden, and eventually to his sluice box on the dry creek below the house. The outdoor toilet was on the opposite side of the house from the animal yards and shed.

Best of all, we had inherited a kangaroo, which Grandpa had raised, and her little joey, still peeking comfortably out of its mother's pouch. Kangaroos are the funniest looking animals I've ever seen. And Joey is a good name for the kangaroo's funny baby.

We ate all our meals in the kitchen, except for when it was warm enough to sit outside on the veranda in the swing near the fruit trees. The kangaroo, which Ma named Hoppy, always waited near the veranda for handouts after supper, then hopped away into the night. On cold nights, Hoppy slept in the shed. My room faced the shed and two yards where Old Lop Ears, Girlie and Bossie, our milk cow, were penned. The pigpen was on the other side of the shed, near the chicken coop.

A week after the big meeting, Ma and Pa made a trip to Omeo for supplies. They took the bullock wagon and dropped me at school on their way. They wouldn't be returning until after dark, so I was going to have to walk home. My black eye was almost gone and my ear was healing. The gang had been really quiet. Mike and Jimmy glared at me a lot, but their glares made their faces look ugly. I really loved my Pa for sticking up for me the way he did.

I had a rabbit skinned and cut up for dinner before Ma and Pa arrived from Omeo. I had picked a wildflower for Ma and had it in a drinking glass on the table. When I heard the wagon stop beside the house, I hurried outside to help carry in the supplies.

"How was school?" Pa asked.

The kangaroos appeared beside the wagon. I petted Hoppy's neck a couple of times and touched little Joey on the top of his head. The baby kangaroo shyly ducked back into its mother's pouch.

"Went okay. No problems. Miss Evans kept an eye on things."

"Maybe things are changin'," Pa said.

Ma stepped down from the wagon, groaning and rubbing the small of her back with both hands. "She's a good teacher," Ma said. "We're lucky to have a schoolhouse nearby."

"Two miles over a hill and across two creeks ain't nearby," I answered.

"It's closer than the ten miles it used to be in Montana," Pa said, handing me a heavy sack of flour. "Take that into the kitchen and bring back an apple for Hoppy."

Pa followed me into the house with a wooden box of groceries and sat it on the table. Ma came in with the second box. "Your chores done, Casey?"

"Yes, Ma'am," I answered. "And I got all the trees watered and filled the tank beside the house."

"I'll put things away while I cook. Thanks for the rabbit. Looks nice and fat. Help your pa settle Girlie in for the evening and bring in a few more sticks of kitchen wood, then wash up for supper."

"Yes, Ma'am," I answered.

"I love the wildflower. Thanks, son."

"You're welcome, Ma." I followed Pa outside.

Pa and I drove the wagon around the yard, parked it beside the shed, and started loosening Girlie's leather traces. Pa was bubbling with excitement. I could tell he had some news, so I stopped what I was doing and leaned on Girlie to listen.

He said, "There's a rodeo in Omeo in three weeks, on Easter Saturday. The day after Easter Monday, the big muster officially starts. That's when the station owners get together to bring their stock out of the high plains. It's goin' to be like the Fourth of July rodeo in Biddle. There's goin' to be bronco ridin', horse races and – you remember how we almost won that sack race last year? Well, they got the same race here, father and son. I entered our names. Thought we could practice runnin' around the shed with that old burlap bag. Have you seen it lately?"

I led Girlie to the yard and tossed her some hay. "They're called hessian bags here, Pa," I said. "It's at school. I used it to carry my bat last week. I'll bring it home tomorrow." Hurrying back to the shed, I asked, "Who else has entered the race?"

"I'm not sure, but there's quite a few on the list. Why?"

"I hope Mike enters! Do you really think we have a chance to win?"

Pa put his arm around my shoulders as we walked

towards the house. "I figure we have a good chance. They don't know how fast we are, us bein' strangers to these parts and all."

———•—•———

Pa and I practiced the hessian bag race around the shed every evening at least twice before dinner. Hoppy and Joey always hopped behind as if we were going on a great adventure. But it wasn't the Omeo Rodeo that held my interest. It was the weekend before the rodeo. I had convinced Ma and Pa to go in search of Moonrunner. I just had to see him again.

But as the weekend approached, I really got worried. It rained all day Friday and kept raining into the night. Early Saturday morning, however, the sun was brilliant.

I quickly did all my chores while Pa packed our camping things on Old Lop Ears. Ma and Pa rode double on Girlie. I sat precariously on top of the mule's pack. We worked our way down Bingo Munjie Creek towards the Mitta Mitta River, along an old cattle trail. There was a chill in the air, a breeze drifting down the canyon that seemed to carry with it the promise of an early winter. We all wore the sheepskin coats that we'd brought with us from Montana. I searched beneath every tree and behind every rock for brumbies as we rode along. There were plenty of kangaroos and wallabies. A noisy flock of white cockatoos scattered as we passed. The wider track suddenly ended at the edge of the Mitta Mitta.

"Looks like the main track goes across," Pa said. He dismounted and walked to the edge of the water. "It don't look none too safe. What do you reckon, Case?"

"It ain't that bad. Look!" I slid down from the mule, yanked off my boots, and waded into flooding river. My plan was to wade all the way across.

Ma went hysterical. "Casey! Get out of the water!"

"Moonrunner's on the other side. We gotta cross." I kept wading.

"Get back here, now!" Ma sounded frantic so I turned around. "We're not crossing that river! And that's all there is to it." Ma almost drowned in the Ohio River when she was a kid. She's been nervous about water ever since.

"Why don't we take the trail along this side of the river where you spotted Moonrunner?" said Pa.

"It's a dead end, don't you remember? Where you found me riding Old Lop Ears was the end of the trail."

"Well, we have a choice," Pa said. "We can either go back home and camp under the fruit trees and listen to Bossie mooin' or find brumbies someplace else."

"But we won't see Moonrunner."

"We'll see him another time when the river's safer to cross." I knew that tone. Ma's words were final.

"Let's turn up the mountain. There's a trail," Pa said. "Looks like brumby country to me."

"It doesn't look possible," Ma answered. She slid down from Girlie and stretched her legs. "Been a while since I've ridden."

The trail up the mountain was steep and slippery with moisture oozing from near-vertical limestone rocks. I was really disappointed about not being able to see Moonrunner and I didn't want to go home. This was our first outing as a family in Australia. It was nice being together. Desperate to keep going instead of turning back, I pulled on my boots and scrambled up the steep slope. Eventually, I found a level area and shouted down, "I think we can make it. It's only rough in the beginning."

We pulled the animals up the mountain for an hour until we reached the top of a broad spur where deep yellow-green grass grew beneath scattered white ribbon gums. A strange bird that sounded like a ringing bell alerted the bush of our intrusion and flew away. We rested Girlie and Lop Ears at the edge of the spur and looked back towards Omeo.

Pa dusted his breeches and said, "Let's take a vote."

"Let's keep going," I said quickly. I shaded my eyes with my hand and squinted at the sun. "It's not even noon yet. We gotta see some brumbies before we eat."

"What if we don't see any?" Pa asked. "Does that mean we don't eat?"

"I'm with Casey," Ma said. "Let's cross this flat area and see what's on the other side. If we don't see any, we'll have lunch."

As we led the animals across, Pa held one hand in the air, a signal for us to stop. He pointed to the ground and whispered, "Horse droppin's. Must be brumbies nearby. It's fresh."

I handed Lop Ears' reins to Ma and ran ahead. "Look, horse tracks!" I whispered loudly.

On the upward side of the long spur the bush became impenetrable. I eventually found a path just down from the crest on the shady side of the spur. Fresh prints could easily be seen. I ran back and whispered, "About a dozen horses." Not waiting for Ma and Pa to follow, I ducked into the bush.

"Can't see a thing," Ma said. She was in front of Pa, pulling Old Lop Ears up the ragged trail.

Ma held up her hand. "Listen!"

The sound of small stones and gravel rolling down the mountain was being carried on the wind.

"Brumbies! It's gotta be brumbies!" I said. The excitement was almost too much for me to handle.

Pa whispered, "Shh! We're gettin' close. Mary, tie Lop Ears to that bush and we'll give chase on foot."

We dodged around ghostly snow gums hanging precariously over the trail. The trail split.

"This way," I whispered loudly, so excited to be this close to wild horses again. "The brumbies came this way," I said. The trail I had chosen was along a narrow incline, barely clinging to the side of the limestone cliff. We worked our way carefully upward, leaping at times across spaces that had no trail at all.

"Casey, look!" Ma touched my arm. "Across the canyon."

Fifteen brumbies fought their way up the face of the steep gorge, trying to reach shelter in the thick snow gums at the top. Their hooves knocked rocks and debris loose behind them. None of the horses was black so I knew that it wasn't Moonrunner's band. A dark bay was in front. She must have been the lead mare, making all the decisions. That's the way it was with broomtails in Montana. The stallion would be somewhere near the back.

"There! Ma, the dark chestnut! That's the stallion." I stood perfectly still, holding a branch away from my face. My heart kept pounding in my ears. I didn't breathe – I couldn't breathe. "Aren't they beautiful?" I said.

Most of the brumbies were chestnut or solid brown. Four were white with large brown patterns on their flanks and front shoulders. One was reddish-brown. I watched without moving. The brumbies reached the top and, like ghosts, quickly blended into the snow gums as if they had never been there.

Ma stood behind me and put her arms around my shoulders. "That was really exciting!"

"Thanks for coming, Ma," I said.

"They're gone," Pa said as he joined us.

"Let's follow them across the gorge," I said, unable to let go so easily.

"It's too rugged," Pa answered. "Besides, the brumbies are long gone. We made enough noise while chasin' 'em to scare a ghost. This country's much different than the box canyons along the Little Powder River. Sound travels. It's real rugged and not as open. We were lucky to see the brumbies at all. We might as well have some lunch."

"Let's camp beside the Bingo Munjie Creek," Ma said. "I saw a flat spot just before we reached the Mitta Mitta."

"Sounds good to me," Pa answered. "The creek ain't muddy like the river. Should be some good fishin'. Maybe have trout for breakfast. What do you think, Case?"

I didn't mind turning back now that I had seen the brumbies. And I knew Pa was right: they'd be long gone for a spell.

Sitting on a rock overlooking the gorge, eating cold sandwiches, I said, "Pa, Lop Ears is getting slower every day as winter approaches. It's taking me twice as long to get to school. I need a horse."

"Maybe in the spring," Pa answered.

Ma was quietly laughing and I wondered why. She said, "It's not getting to school you're worried about, it's chasing those brumbies. Your eyes are really sparkling for the first time since we arrived in Australia."

★ CHAPTER FIVE ★

Lady

I'd been looking forward to the Omeo Rodeo all week. I was hoping it'd be as exciting as the Fourth of July picnic in Biddle. Families from all over the high plains would be there – maybe I'd make some new friends.

We left home early because Ma was determined to win a blue ribbon for her buttered sweet potatoes and her deep-dish apple pie. Pa entered a five-foot long wooden chain he'd carved from a single piece of California redwood during our ocean voyage from San Francisco.

We wandered around the central tent where all the handicrafts were on display, admiring all the homemade items. Or rather Ma and Pa did – I kept busy by eating any free samples I could get my hands on.

About an hour went by before an announcer held a megaphone to his mouth and yelled, "It's time for the hessian bag race! All teams to the starting line!"

I ran to our wagon to get the hessian bag. When I returned, I saw that Mike and his father already had a leg each inside their bag. Frank and his father were just slipping a bag over their ankles when they fell. They laughed loudly and finished the job sitting down. It surprised me to see that Frank was actually human.

Jimmy and Charlie hadn't entered the race, but I spotted them standing together at the finish line, glaring at me. I made a face at them and turned away.

"Sit, quick!" Pa said, "On that rock." He tied our legs together with strips of cloth from a torn shirt so we would run as a team and slipped on the hessian bag. We hobbled to the starting line. I glanced up and down the line at the other teams, each crouched in anticipation of the starting gun. I glared at Mike without smiling, wishing he would fall on his face.

"Everybody ready?" the starter barked. I felt Pa's arm tighten around my shoulders. We had practiced our starting move over and over because, according to Pa, the first leap is what wins the race. When the gun sounded, our tied-together legs went first, then we powered our other legs around and threw the bagged legs forward again. Pa and I were hitting every step in unison. I knew we were winning and turned to see how far behind Mike was.

"Don't look back!" Pa yelled between strides. "You might fall. Just keep runnin' – like you was chasin' Moonrunner!"

I caught my big toe on the hessian bag and slammed to the ground, pulling Pa down with me. Trying to get up, we fell down again. We finally regained our balance in time to watch the end of the race. I was mortified.

"I'm sorry, Pa. We were ahead!"

When the judge presented the blue ribbon to Mike and his father, I blew up.

"It's not fair!" I shouted. "We were better than they were!" I hobbled over to the judge, dragging Pa with me. "Let's race again. I tripped. It's not fair!"

"Go home, cheater Yank. You lost!" Charlie sneered.

The judge shrugged. "I'm sorry, son, that's part of the race. Better luck next year."

"My pa and me challenge Mike Carson and his pa, and Frank Howard and his pa to another race around the rodeo yard."

I felt Pa's calloused hands on my shoulders. "We lost, Case. Let it be."

"We can beat 'em. They're chicken, that's all."

The judge said, "Easy, son. It's not polite calling anyone names, especially in Omeo."

Mike's father said, "I accept the challenge. What do you say, Dan? Feel like another race?"

Pa shrugged. "All the way around the rodeo yard this time?"

"Sure, why not?"

The judge yelled, "Folks! We've got a challenge! The Jenners have challenged the Carsons and Howards. Clear the way. We've got a challenge!"

Pa stuck his hand out in front of Mr. Carson and said, "Good luck, Jack." They shook hands. Then Pa shook hands with Mr. Howard and said, "Good luck, Joseph."

"Call me Joe," Mr. Howard answered. "And good luck to you and Casey."

The three teams lined up on a line drawn along the ground. Pa and me were in the middle. The judge fired his pistol. We surged ahead. I concentrated on the rhythm of each stride this time, without looking back. Out of the corner of my eye, I saw Mike and his father fall at the first turn. They quickly scrambled to their feet and kept running. Frank and his father made it to the final turn before they tumbled to the ground. I knew we were going to win. All we had to do was to keep from falling just a little longer. Pa suddenly tripped on a blue gum root. Staggering, I managed to keep Pa from falling, but we lost our rhythm and the other teams caught up. We were all running neck and neck. It was anybody's race.

I felt a surge of power coming from Pa and I lengthened my stride to match. I tightened my grip around Pa's waist. Pa tightened his grip around my shoulders.

We were in perfect balance, taking gigantic strides, literally pulling ourselves away from the other racers and towards the finish line. Just two more leaps. One more! We surged across. We had won!

The judge said, "There aren't any ribbons for winning challenges, but we'd all like to know how you ran so fast, especially at the end."

Pa smiled and glanced at me. "Well, that's simple." I watched the other fathers lean forward and wait for Pa to divulge our secret. I didn't know what Pa was going to say so I was just as interested as everyone else. "We just think about a big bowl of ice cream waitin' for us at the finish line. Right, Casey?"

"Yeah, chocolate," I replied. Everyone laughed loudly. We hobbled over to find Ma beaming happily.

"That was a good race! You two ran like scared rabbits! When you almost fell there at the end, I thought you'd lost for sure. But you beat those other two by a mile," she said.

Pa asked, "How'd you know we'd win, Case?"

"'Cause we've been practicing going around the shed. I figured the others had practiced in a straight line. It's much more difficult running in circles."

"That's true in life, too, son," Pa answered.

Ma said, "I'm so proud of you both!"

"Thanks, Ma," I answered, grinning broadly.

Pa untied our legs and stood. "Buckjumpin' the wild brumby is next. We'd better hurry to get good seats. After that, it's the horserace."

"A quarter mile?" I asked.

"Half," Pa answered. "I don't think they run the quarter in Omeo."

Mr. Wallace, a storekeeper who knew Pa and Ma from

trading in Omeo, sat next to us. Thank goodness he was there, because the rules, like everything else in Australia, were very confusing. Mr. Wallace explained the event and I listened.

"The day before the rodeo, some brumby-runners from the Cobungra Station are assigned the task of catching a mob of wild brumbies. They've never been ridden. For this event, two buckjumpers are matched against one wild brumby. They must rope, saddle and ride the brumby before they get their teeth kicked out or ribs broken. One buckjumper ropes and the other cinches on a saddle and rides."

I reckoned the event to be a cross between calf roping and bronco riding in Montana. It was my first look at the toughness and daring of the high plains brumby-runners and buckjumpers. They didn't appear to have any fear. I was amazed to watch one buckjumper put his arms and legs around the wild horse's neck and dangle beneath as it bucked around the yard, slowing it down long enough for his partner to get up from being piled into the dirt and get back on the critter. That team, to the applause of the audience, won the event hands down.

When it was over, Pa thanked Mr. Wallace and patted me on the back. "Come on, son, let's hurry down and pick a winner before the horserace begins."

More than twenty horses were warming up for the half mile race. As I stood beside Pa, I imagined myself mounted on each horse, riding it to victory. The small mare I picked to win suddenly stopped in front of Pa.

I jumped back as a voice boomed down, "Hey, Jenner. Why don't you enter your mule?"

I looked up to see a round face grinning down at us. It was Mr. Parkes, the wealthiest station owner in the area. Several men around me laughed. "We'll give you a quarter mile head start. In a half mile race, that isn't bad." There was more laughter, this time louder.

"No, thanks," Pa answered politely, "I'd hate to beat you boys out of your money." He petted Mr. Parkes' mare on the neck. "Pretty small to be racin', ain't she?"

"That's what I told Ernie," Mr. Parkes said. "But my foreman says she's the fastest runner I own. He's riding Diablo, another horse of mine." Mr. Parkes pointed at a frisky dark bay. "Now, that's a horse! I entered two this year, just in case. Haven't had anyone beat me in this race for five years. I own the best horses in the territory."

"And the most, probably," Pa added.

While the conversation between Pa and Mr. Parkes continued, I was admiring the small mare. She was a sorrel, with four perfectly matched stockings, a white blaze on her face and a long red mane and tail. The mare was built differently from the other horses in the race. She was long legged and slim while the others were stocky and muscular. I petted her pink nose and rubbed her trim neck as I dreamed of riding her to find Moonrunner.

"Like her, do you, son?" Mr. Parkes asked. His booming voice startled me.

"Yes, sir. She's sure pretty. If I ever get me a riding horse again, she's going to be just like – what's her name, sir?"

"Lady."

"Lady. It's a nice name for her, sir."

"There's no sense wishin', son," Pa said. "Now, stand back and let Mr. Parkes get to the startin' line."

"See ya, Jenner." Mr. Parkes reined Lady around on the grass and spurred her into a trot.

I watched, still half-dreaming. "She sure is beautiful, ain't she, Pa?"

"Is that your choice?"

"Yes, sir! I think Lady will outrun them all."

"Okay, I'll bet on Diablo, the one Ernie's ridin'."

We watched the judge climb to his platform and yell, "Clear the raceway. Everyone clear the raceway. The race is a half mile this year, so I'll have no complaining about not being told. Now! There'll be no shoving, kicking, or trying to knock each other off stride like you did last year. If you cross the starting line before the gun goes off, you'll be eliminated and forfeit your entry fee. Any questions?" After waiting for the stragglers to get in position, the judge yelled, "Riders, to the starting line and listen for the gun." My eyes were on Lady.

When the gun fired, twenty-three horses thundered down the long straight-of-way directly at us. Diablo was clearly in front. Eventually I spotted Lady at the very back. She finished last.

Mr. Parkes was furious. He angrily reined Lady around in tight circles. "I'm going to shoot you, you no-good piece of horse flesh!" He spurred her with contempt and leaped to the ground.

"Pa, he's kickin' her in the stomach!" I yelled. I ran towards Lady, not knowing what I was going to do, but knowing I had to do something. Mr. Parkes kicked her again. Lady tried to get away, but couldn't escape the iron grip on her reins.

"Don't kick her, sir!" I yelled. "It wasn't her fault." I tried to place myself between Mr. Parkes and Lady to protect her, but he pushed me aside.

"Get out of here, boy! This' none of your business!"

Lady spun away just as Mr. Parkes kicked again. He missed and fell on his back. Getting to his feet, he punched Lady in the nose with his fist. "That'll teach you! Ernie! Get my rifle!"

"Don't shoot her, don't shoot her! Please, don't shoot her," I pleaded. "I'll buy her from you."

Mr. Parkes looked at me and sneered. "Your pa can't even buy a new mule, let alone a horse. Now get back and stop pestering me!"

"I'll work for her," I yelled back.

"What about your chores at home, son?" Pa asked.

"I'll do them at night," I answered.

"You know that won't work, Casey. You need daylight to do your chores."

Mr. Parkes must've regained control of his temper because what he said next really surprised me. "Tell you what I'll do, boy. The muster starts on Tuesday. Most of my station hands will be up in the high plains for a month or so. Work for me on the muster during your school holiday and useless Lady here is yours."

"Do you mean it, really?" I felt my face glowing with excitement. "I can't wait to –"

"You can't go on the muster, son. I'm countin' on your help with the hay, and stockpilin' wood for winter."

Mr. Parkes said, "Jenner, I've no use for this horse now that I know she can't run. Be reasonable! If you're willing to let – what's your name, boy?"

"Casey, sir."

"If you're willing to let Casey work at my station from sunup till dark, three days a week during the muster, Lady will be his and he doesn't have to ride that dumb mule. That's got to be embarrassing for the lad."

"Then I can work at home, too. Please, Pa."

"You'll be doin' double chores, son, and …" Pa paused and I knew I had him.

"And what!" I hurried Pa's words. "And what, Pa?"

"And …" Pa hesitated. "We'll have to ask your ma."

Ma had been listening. She said, "It's okay with me, if it's okay with your pa."

"Yahoo!" I screamed wildly. Knowing she would be frightened of being touched on her nose after being hit, I tenderly stroked Lady's shoulder and put my head tightly against her neck to make sure she was real. I couldn't believe she was going to be mine.

"That settles it," Mr. Parkes said. "Casey, be at my station at first light on Tuesday. Ernie runs things while I'm on the muster. If Ernie tells me that you did a good job, Lady's yours. And you might as well take Lady home now and ride her while you're working for me. You'll need to find yourself a saddle, because mine is not part of the deal." He tied Lady to his buggy and loosened her girth.

"Any saddle's fine with me!" I said. My heart beat wildly. I was already in love with Lady.

"Any saddle *isn't* fine," Mr. Parkes said. "Your saddle's got to fit your behind, because you'll be spending a lot of time sitting." Mr. Parkes pulled his saddle from Lady and placed it carefully on the back of the buggy. He untied Lady's reins and handed them to me. "You can keep the bridle. It's too small for any of my other horses. I'll see you first thing Tuesday morning."

★ CHAPTER SIX ★

Pa's Worry

I led Lady to the family wagon and tenderly stroked her neck as I tied her to the rail.

"Easy, girl," I said softly. "You're mine now. Nobody's going to hurt you. You're safe with me. I'll take good care of you." She was still quivering from Mr. Parkes' rough treatment. "I'm worried, Pa. Lady's not hurt, is she?"

Pa examined her stomach and legs, felt her tender nose and checked for bleeding. "I don't believe so, son. She looks fine. Just scared. Leave her tied here while we eat. You can ride her home."

From that moment on, the rodeo really dragged. I couldn't sit still. I kept glancing towards the bullock wagon to see if Lady was still there, hardly believing she was real. I was proud to own Lady and proud of myself for protecting her.

I gulped only one piece of chocolate cake and none of Ma's apple pie. And I rushed Ma and Pa through the barbecue. Pa finally decided it was time to head home.

Pa held Lady's reins near the bit while I jumped into the wagon and gently climbed on her back. She didn't move. I think she must've felt how much I already loved her. The softness of her bare back on my legs was a marvelous feeling. My body tingled with delight. Such a beautiful horse and she was mine. Mine! I couldn't believe my good fortune. I looked down at Ma and Pa.

"My first horse in Australia! Isn't she proud?"

When Ma laughs, sometimes, I feel it right in my heart. That's how she laughed now, kinda light and merry with a twinkle in her eye.

"You both look proud to me," she said. "Do you like her as much as you liked Arrowhead?"

"Of course! Lady is absolutely beautiful."

When Pa handed me the reins, my pent-up emotions exploded. I yelled as loudly as I could and galloped around the racecourse. Pa turned the bullock wagon across the rodeo grounds for home. I galloped by, yelling like a warrior on an Indian raiding party, and circled the wagon several times, pretending to shoot a bow and arrow. Several families had stopped to watch me ride so I was putting on a show, riding bareback using my knees and no hands.

Pa yelled, "Better give her a rest, son. She's already had one race today, she doesn't need another."

"Okay, Pa."

He stopped the wagon. I dismounted and tied Lady to the side railing. Lowering the tailgate, I sat backwards with my feet dangling over the edge, watching Lady. Pa made a snicking sound and popped the reins. "Giddy up, Girlie. Let's go home." The family mare pulled the wagon northward, around the hill out of Omeo and down the winding road that followed Livingston Creek.

Ma suddenly said, "We have to go back."

"Why?" Pa asked.

"You forgot to pick up your carved wooden chain."

Pa smiled and said, "Casey, look beneath the seat."

I unrolled a rag rug and held it up for Ma to see. It was made out of pieces of colorful cloth braided and sewn together in spiraling coils.

"I saw you admirin' that rug when I was talkin' with the librarian about books for Casey. It's about the right size for your kitchen so I traded the wooden chain for it."

"That's really nice," Ma said, "It'll keep my feet warm this winter."

I left it unrolled and lay down so I could see Lady walking behind the wagon. I was planning my first trip to find Moonrunner.

On Monday evening, the day before I was to work for Mr. Parkes, after I finished my chores and bedded Lady down for the night, we sat on the front veranda, talking about the rodeo. Pa had won a blue ribbon for his wood carving and Ma's deep-dish apple pie won a separate award for excellence since it had been the only apple pie entry. Pa emptied the burned tobacco from his pipe by tapping it gently on the veranda railing and placed the pipe carefully in his pocket.

"I love the large sound of the night birds in Australia," Ma said.

Hoppy must have heard us talking or smelled Pa's pipe smoke because she appeared looking for a handout. Joey decided he wasn't getting his share of the food inside the pouch and climbed out. I couldn't help but laugh, watching the little kangaroo hop around. I broke a carrot in two, tossed the large piece to Hoppy, and carefully handed the smaller piece to Joey. Instead of taking the carrot, the little joey dived back into the pouch with only his tail showing. There was absolutely nothing like that back in Montana.

Pa asked, "What time are you leavin', son?"

"The station is about half an hour's ride from here, up Connleys Road," I answered. I tossed the rest of the carrot to Hoppy. "Mr. Parkes wants me there by sunup."

"That's half an hour in daylight. You'd better leave early."

"What about breakfast? You can't work all day without eating," Ma said.

"I'll take a couple of leftover scones and beef jerky," I answered. My boots felt uncomfortable so I yanked them off and tossed them across the veranda towards the front door.

"What kind of work you reckon I'll be doing?"

"Probably the same as here: cleanin' sheds, milkin', feedin' the livestock around the station while the other hands are on the muster. Maybe help the cook."

"I hope not! Those are chores, not work," I said. "I want to do something else."

"Work is work, son, whether it's chores or not."

"On other stations, they hire swagmen to do the chores, or they have big families to share the chores."

"Without your help, son, it'd be real difficult handling this place," Ma said. "I'm doing all I can, and your Pa's certainly doing all he can. Whatever's left is yours to do. Now, let's get inside before this chill reaches our bones."

When Pa says to do something, most of the time we do it, but we always do what Ma says. So I patted Hoppy a final time, picked up my boots, and opened the front door.

"It's just that I'd like to do something interesting for a change instead of chores. I'm tired of choppin' wood."

Pa carried in two pieces of firewood and dropped them onto the low-burning fire. I waited for Ma and closed the door behind me. Pa stoked the fire with an iron. "You made the deal with Mr. Parkes. Besides, maybe he'll have you cuttin' a different kinda wood."

"At least softer," I laughed. I decided to drop my complaining about chores. Owning Lady would be worth the extra work, whether it was chores or not. I tossed my boots towards my room and sat down on the floor in front of the fireplace. "Don't worry, Pa. I'll work double hard on the three days I'm home. Even on Sunday to catch up, if I have to."

Ma sat in her rocker and pulled a shawl around her shoulders while Pa lit the lantern. "Nobody works on Sunday, except me doing a little cooking," she said. She started the chair rocking. "A body has to rest once a week to build strength for the next week."

"Your ma's right. On Sunday, you and Lady are on your own."

Ma said, "Now, Casey, get to bed. It's already late, and you have to get up early. The biscuits will be sitting on the stove with some corned beef."

I kissed her goodnight on the cheek and said, "Scones, Ma. They're called scones here."

"I've been making biscuits all my life and I swear I'll never call them anything else," she answered. "Or at least not for a while, anyway."

Pa chuckled. I glanced at him to see if I could stay up longer, but he was already lost in thought, whittling on a new piece of wood. He held a worried look on his face that troubled me. I couldn't place it, but I'd seen that look before. Was it last winter in Biddle?

"Think I'll go check on Lady real quick before I go to bed," I said, picking up my boots.

Pa looked up from his whittling. "Don't bother, son. She'll be fine. I'll check on her myself before I go to bed. Now, do as your ma done said. Get to bed!"

"Yes, sir." I went into my room, closed the door and stood at the window, watching Lady walk around her strange yard. I could hear my parents talking from the next room.

The rocker stopped squeaking. "You have to tell Casey," Ma said. "It isn't fair not to tell him."

"Everythin'll be fine, dear, don't worry."

"You coming to bed?"

"Not just yet. I've got some thinkin' to do."

I stayed at the window for a long time, wondering what Pa had to tell me. After a while, I heard the front door close and watched Pa check on Lady. But I remained standing in the shadows at the window so he wouldn't see me. After Pa went inside, I leaned out the window and watched Lady slowly walking around inside the yard. I whistled softly like I used to with Arrowhead, but Lady just kept walking.

"This Sunday, Lady, we'll go find Moonrunner," I whispered. "We'll both make him our friend."

I knew that I had to get some rest. Forcing myself to put on my pajamas, I crawled under the covers, but Moonrunner galloped into my mind as soon as I closed my eyes, running beside Lady. Both horses stopped in front of me. I gave each a lump of sugar. All three of us walked to a spring where I stretched out on the grass to sleep.

★ CHAPTER SEVEN ★

I'm a Buckrunner

On Tuesday morning, the beginning of my cattle-muster holiday, I arrived at Mr. Parkes' station riding Lady bareback. As I rode up, a Chinese cook, standing on the cookhouse veranda, beat on a large steel bar bent into a triangle. Station hands came running from all directions. I tied Lady to the hitching rail alongside several dozen other horses and waited for Mr. Parkes to arrive.

He stepped from the main house, glanced at the clear skies, smiled and strode towards me. "How's Lady doing?" he asked.

Lady spotted Mr. Parkes and started quivering. Her eyes went wild. She tried to break away. I wasn't able to calm her so I hurried towards Mr. Parkes to keep him from getting any closer. "She's settled down," I answered. Trying to take the edge off my nervousness, I added, "And she's a lot easier to ride than Old Lop Ears."

"I'm glad you're on time. Had breakfast?" he asked.

"A scone and some corned beef on the way over," I said.

"As long as you work for me and get here early, you might as well eat with the station hands. Come on, let's find Ernie." I followed Mr. Parkes into the crowded cookhouse. It was a large, smoke-filled room with two cook stoves at the far end and a long, narrow eating table running down the middle. The station hands, with their floppy hats hanging on pegs behind them, were already eating. Mr. Parkes led me around the table to the far side of the room.

"Ernie, this' the Jenner boy I told you about. He's yours three days a week for the next three weeks, so work him like one of the hands."

Mr. Parkes left the cookhouse as Ernie scooted over to make room. "Sit down, mate. What's your name?"

"Casey Jenner," I answered, lowering my voice to make me sound older.

"Well, Casey, just a minute, I'll tell the cook to bring you some tucker."

The cook banged a tin plate full of potatoes, fried eggs and steak and a mug of very hot billy tea in front of me. There was already a half loaf of damper on the table with a large knife stuck in the side.

"Better let it cool a little," Ernie said, pointing to the tea.

"Take milk?"

"Not with tea," I answered. I watched the other station hands gulp the hot billy tea. Eventually, I sipped my tea and almost vomited.

Ernie smiled at my discomfort and said, "This cook makes the worst billy tea in the territory."

"I reckon he does," I answered, holding my mug with one hand, trying to decide if I should try another sip. "We drink coffee at home. Pa brought a big bag of beans from San Francisco."

"I don't think it'd hurt the cook's feelings if you didn't drink any more," Ernie said. "One time, I poured a cup of tea on some wild flowers. By the end of the week, all the flowers were dead." Several station hands near Ernie laughed. I laughed with them and shoved the tea into the middle of the table next to the damper. "How about some fresh milk?" said Ernie. "The cook always has extra milk in the cool box."

After breakfast, Ernie remained talking with me while the other men gathered their things in preparation for leaving on the muster.

"Where you from, Casey?"

"Montana. We just got here last Christmas, barely in time to get the planting done."

"Your father a farmer?"

"Mostly."

"How'd you ever talk Mr. Parkes out of Lady?"

"She lost the race, so he didn't want her anymore. He

wanted to shoot her."

"The boss has a bad temper. Just have to wait until he cools down to reason with him. Lady was the fastest horse he owned, so I thought she'd do better in the race. He sure was mad at me for a while. But he should've kept her for next year."

"Why?" I asked. "If she lost once, she'll lose again."

"Next year is the two mile race."

"I didn't pay much attention to the race. It could've been ten miles and I'd never have known. I was watching Lady."

Ernie laughed and said, "Really like her, do ya?"

"Best thing that ever happened to me."

"Well, take care of her and she'll take care of you. Lady's a young mare with lots of sense. I've ridden her several times. She's a distance runner. If you ever want her to run, give Lady her head. When she gets running all out, with her belly almost dragging the ground, watch out! She's hard to turn."

"What do I do?" I asked.

"Not much you can do. Just hang on until she slows down."

"I'll be careful," I answered.

The cookhouse was suddenly empty. Ernie put on his hat and went outside, carrying a coiled piece of braided leather. I followed, admiring the unusual handle.

"What's the whip for?" I asked.

"You never go into the bush without a stockwhip." Ernie handed it to me. It felt heavy, not like a coiled rope at all. "Lots of snakes in the bush, all poisonous, so be careful." He took the whip from my hand, uncoiled it, and said, "It's made of tightly braided greenhide. Stand back and let me show you how it's done." Ernie swung the whip around several times before snapping the single leather tip. It sounded exactly like Pa's Winchester rifle.

"Wow! Can I try?"

"Sure. Have a go."

I twirled the stockwhip around and around, trying to imitate Ernie, but when I tried to make it pop, the long whip caught me behind the head and wrapped around my throat. It really stung. I felt a large welt appear on the side of my face.

Ernie laughed. "Need a little practice, I'd say. But it's much easier to handle on horseback." He coiled the stockwhip and tied it to his belt. "Buckjumpers always carry stockwhips to chase brumbies and scare off wild animals. Cattlemen crack the stockwhip to keep the cattle moving. But I reckon the less the whip is cracked, the calmer the cattle."

"Cowboys in Montana shoot pistols in the air and shout to keep cattle moving," I said.

"A stockwhip sounds like a pistol shot," Ernie said, "and it's much cheaper than bullets."

We watched until the hands leaving on the muster were out of sight. The remaining station hands walked their horses over to await Ernie's instructions. I noticed they were all carrying axes.

Ernie said, "You boys ride ahead and start cutting brush. You know where to go. Casey and me will be there shortly."

The hands trotted through the entrance gate and turned towards Mount Worchester.

"Ever been buckrunning?"

"N-no, I can't say that I have," I stammered. "What's buckrunning? Does it have something to do with brumbies?"

"It's what I think you'd call mustanging in America."

I was suddenly excited. I wouldn't be doing chores after all! "I've chased mustangs in Montana, but never caught any," I said.

Ernie nodded. "Might be a little different here. Where's your saddle?"

"Don't need one," I answered.

"You do if you're going to chase wild brumbies through the woolly butts," Ernie said.

"Haven't had a chance to get one."

"Come on, I've got an old Sealey saddle and blanket in the shed you can have."

Half an hour later, Ernie and I rode away from the station. As we rode, Ernie demonstrated how to crack the stockwhip from the saddle. He let me try several times, but it was much more difficult than it looked. I wasn't strong enough to make it snap properly. I handed it back to Ernie. He coiled the whip, tied it to his saddle, and waited for me to ride beside him.

"There's three ways to catch brumbies," said Ernie. "Two men on horseback chase a wild buck up a mountain. The brumbies don't have much wind, so they tire easily. One of the riders grabs the brumby by the tail to slow it down while the other rider drops a rope around its neck."

"The wild broomtails in Montana can outrun any horse across the prairie. Must be a different breed," I said.

"Maybe. But the other way to catch bucks is to set traps made out of trees and brush way out in the bush. When a buck enters the trap, it hits the trigger and the gate slams shut. But I don't like that method because too many good horses are killed going wild inside the trap until the trappers eventually return days later to take them out."

"What do you do?" I asked.

"I build a trap in a large boxed gully, one where I know there's no escape. And I make sure the boxed end of the gully is flat."

"Why?" I asked.

"If the floor of the gully is sloped, the bucks will pack together on the downhill side of the trap and hurt each other."

We rode silently for a while and watched the sun come up over Mount Sam. I wondered how Ernie had become so smart. I really started liking him. As we turned up the mountain, he said, "Today we're going to barricade the boxed end of a gully with brush. Then we'll build a trapdoor for the brumbies to enter. Tomorrow, when you're not here, my boys'll make a funnel out of brush that'll extend from the mouth of the gully and narrow towards the trapdoor. The funnel forces the bucks into the trap. When they're all inside, the gate man, who has been hiding in the bush beside the trapdoor, releases the rope and a canvas sheet rolls down to cover the exit. The brumbies think the canvas is a solid wall."

"Wow!" I said. "It sounds easy."

"It's not that easy! Everything has to be well planned. Once the bucks know they're trapped, they'll turn and run for the exit. If the canvas isn't down, they'll all get away. The man at the gate has to release the canvas just right. Not too soon, not too late."

"Who's going to be the gate man?" I asked.

"Figured that'd be a good job for you when you come back on Thursday," Ernie said, smiling at me. "So get here early." He put his horse into a lope to catch the other riders.

———◆◆———

After cutting and dragging brush all day, I arrived home after dark completely exhausted. I walked Lady to the shed, unsaddled her and turned her loose in the yard. The hollow sound of my steps on the veranda felt comforting. I caught a glimpse of Hoppy and Joey standing on the edge of the lantern light, curiously watching, but I was too tired to say hello. I opened the door and entered.

Pa looked up from his carving and said, "Evening, son, how'd it go?" He placed his pipe carefully on the mantle.

I managed to grunt hello and flopped in Ma's rocking chair, leaving my boots on. I closed my eyes without saying another word. The squeaking of the old chair slowly rocking back and forth and my unusual silence must have been too much for Ma to endure. She yelled from the kitchen, "Well, how'd it go today, son?"

"Fine," I answered. I finally pulled off my boots and threw them towards my room. A bare toe stuck through a hole in my sock.

"What kind of work did Mr. Parkes have you doin'?" Pa asked.

"I didn't work for Mr. Parkes. I worked for Ernie, the foreman. He's the man that rode Diablo and won the race."

"What doin'?"

"Buckrunning."

Ma wiped her hands on her apron and joined us in the sitting room. She sat down on the old sofa that used to belong to my grandfather. "You mean he had you and Lady galloping in and out of those canyons, chasing those fool brumbies?"

"The only time I got to ride Lady was up towards Mount Worchester and back. We cut and dragged brush all day for the trap."

"Let's see your hands." She pried my hands open. "Just look at those blisters!"

"Better wear gloves next time," Pa said. "I have an extra pair in the shed."

"The station hands don't wear gloves," I answered.

"They're used to that kind of work. You ain't."

"Well, I fixed a big supper and the water's heating out back for a hot bath. The table's set. Let's eat," Ma said. "I'll put some salve on your hands before bedtime."

"How does Lady ride?" Pa asked as he sat down at the table.

"Like a dream!" The tiredness left my body. "Do you know what Ernie said?" I didn't wait for an answer. "He says Lady is a long distance runner. That's why he told Mr. Parkes she was so fast. Says no horse in the area can outrun her."

I realized I was talking faster and faster, gnawing an ear of corn while I spoke, but I couldn't help myself. I was hungry, but I had a lot to say. "Only thing is though," I pointed absentmindedly at Pa with my corncob. "Only thing is," I swallowed, trying to speak, "is that once she gets goin' in a straight line, runnin' all out, she's hard to turn." Pa was smiling. I said, "You know, next year –" I opened my mouth and stuffed in meat and potatoes, and started talking again with my mouth full.

"Son," Ma said. "Either talk or eat, but don't do both at the same time."

"Yes'm." I quickly chewed and swallowed. "Next Omeo Rodeo is going to be the two mile race. I'm going to enter Lady."

"It takes a pound entry fee. That's a lot of money. Where you plan on gettin' that much?" Pa asked.

"I don't know. It's a long time till then. I'll think of somethin'."

"Maybe you can trap this winter," Ma suggested. "I saw fur gloves, hats and boots being sold in Omeo last Saturday. Your grandfather left a dozen traps hanging in the shed. There's some old hides still tacked to the side of the shed. And your pa used to trap in Kentucky when he was a boy."

"Did you, Pa?"

"That was years ago. I was too busy tryin' to make a go of the place in Montana to do any trappin' there. We'll give a look at the traps tomorrow. Probably pretty rusty by now."

Pa's plate was empty so I passed the steaming food across the table. I said, "Ernie gave me an old saddle. It really fits me."

"That was awfully nice of him," Ma said.

"Ernie sounds like a good man to work for," Pa added.

"He sure is. He taught me to crack a whip. I really like him. Besides, he doesn't have me cutting firewood."

Pa laughed and said, "We'll look at that saddle tomorrow. Maybe we can fix it, if it needs fixin'."

"When I win the race, I'll buy a new one, bridle too."

"I told you before, son. Don't dream so big. Then you won't get hurt."

Regardless of Pa's words, in my mind, Lady had already won the race.

Two days later, Ernie and I were standing in front of the brumby trap. Ernie said, "Hide in there and don't move a muscle. Brumbies have real sharp eyes. If they see any movement at all, they'll turn and run the other way."

I stepped into the small, concealed area and Ernie handed me the trigger rope.

"Now, here's what we're going to do," Ernie carried a

piece of brush over to conceal me from the brumbies' eyes. "Yesterday, I spotted a large mob of brumbies a little way from here. It'll be tough getting them this far because of the rugged woolly butt and scrub."

"So how you plan on doing it?" I asked. I could barely see Ernie through the brush.

"I have the station hands staked out for the chase. We crack our stockwhips and force the brumbies to run in one direction only. We keep that up until the brumbies arrive here. Then you take over. Think you can handle it?"

"Sure," I answered. "Just bring 'em on."

"It might take all day, so don't come out until I yell."

By late afternoon, my legs were cramped and I was hungry. I had been hidden all day. I had looked down the gully for the brumbies so many times my eyes hurt. And, to make things worse, I was thirsty. I tried to stand to stretch my legs, but wasn't able to move. I was about to shove the brush aside for a short rest when I heard a voice being carried on the wind. I listened, but heard nothing more. Then I heard the cracking of whips and felt the ground rumbling. It seemed like forever before I saw wild horses thundering towards me.

The entire gully was suddenly alive with bellowing, angry, wild brumbies, running blindly, directly at me. I braced myself as the wild horses funneled through the narrow opening. Pa had told me stories about men being trampled in stampedes. When the wild horses jammed through the gate, their deadly hooves were only three feet away from my head. It seemed hours before Ernie yelled, "Now, Casey! Drop the canvas!"

I released the rope. The canvas didn't fall. I shook the rope violently. Still nothing. "Ernie! It won't drop!" I shouted.

"They'll get away!" someone yelled.

I fought my way out of the brush enclosure. At that moment the horses turned as one and galloped towards the gate. It was a race. The brumby-runners were yelling and frantically cracking their whips, trying to turn the brumbies around. But nothing was going to stop them. I clawed my way to the top of the pole just as the first brumby reached the trapdoor. I yanked the rope. It wouldn't move! I yanked harder. The canvas dropped violently. The force knocked my legs loose and left me dangling by one arm. Angry brumbies bellowed below me. I felt my hand slipping. I knew I was a goner. Ernie galloped across just in time and pulled me onto the back of his horse.

"That was a close one," Ernie said, grinning. "Did you have a chance to count them?"

I had been fighting for my life and Ernie wanted me to count the brumbies? Then I saw the teasing look in his eyes. "Sure did," I answered. "There were four stallions, thirty-three mares, eight colts and ten fillies."

Ernie laughed and gave me an extra-hard toss from the back of his horse. I banged against a gum tree and slid slowly to the ground with my eyes crossed, pretending to be hurt.

I was a buckrunner.

★ CHAPTER EIGHT ★

The Hidden Gorge

Early Sunday morning, before searching for Moonrunner, there was something I had to do.

I approached my grandfather's grave on the hillside beneath the large blue gum tree behind our house, carrying a canning jar tightly in one hand and a shovel in the other. Ma and Pa were still in bed. Pausing beside the grave, I read the epitaph that someone had carved on a wooden plank.

> *Far, far away from his hometown*
> *Sam Jenner lies here face down*
> *Still digging this barren ground*
> *Searching for gold he never found.*

I dropped to both knees beside the grave and said, "Hello, Grandpa, this is your grandson, Casey. I want you to take care of something for me." I held the canning jar above the grave. "It's a photograph of my baseball team. I won't need it anymore, 'cause, just like you, I've decided to start a new life here in Australia. I have a beautiful horse named Lady. You'd like her, Grandpa. And I'm working like a man, chasin' brumbies."

I dug a small hole beside the grave and dropped the jar into the hole. As I slowly covered it, I added, "But I've been wonderin', Grandpa, did you ever get very lonely here in Australia all by yourself? Did you forget what Grandma looked like? And did you ever wonder what my pa looked like when he was growing up? Or did you never really forget them at all and your heart ached so badly that you just gave up and died? That's what I'd like to believe; you just died because you missed them so badly.

Or were you a cheat and crook, like they say? Is that the reason you never came back to America? I wish you could talk, 'cause you left me with an awful burden to carry. They're makin' fun of me at school. Anyway, Grandpa, take care of my buddies. I gotta let them go if I'm gonna fit in to this new world. Thanks, Grandpa. I knew you'd understand."

I leaned on the shovel and looked down at the grave. There was something else on my mind that needed to be said. "Grandpa? One more thing, if you're still listenin'. I wish that I'd known you a little before you died 'cause I don't think Ma and Pa really understand how lonely I've been. Knowing how you survived being alone in Australia would really help."

I quickly fed all the animals, saddled Lady and led her to the house. Pa was sitting on the far end of the veranda trying to make friends with little Joey in the early morning light. Ma was sitting in the veranda swing. "You're up early," she said.

"Had somethin' to do," I answered as I tied Lady to the railing.

"I've got breakfast ready, and made you a lunch."

"Thanks, Ma." I opened the door and held it for Ma and Pa. Sitting at the table, Pa asked, "Where you headed, son?"

"To the Mitta Mitta. I'm riding back to where I saw Moonrunner. Why?" I was hoping he wasn't going to stop me from going.

"If you don't return before dark, I'll know where to look for you."

"Don't worry about me. I'll be back long before supper. And you too, Ma. Don't worry a hole in your new kitchen rug."

"Are you going to cross the Mitta Mitta?" Ma asked.

Danged me! There was no way to find Moonrunner without crossing the river. Knowing how much Ma would worry, I answered very carefully. "It hasn't rained for a long time, Ma. The river will be easy to cross."

"I know you can take care of yourself, Casey," Ma answered. She carried over hot biscuits and beef jerky gravy and set them on the table. "Your pa taught you well. It's just natural for mothers to worry."

"I know you'll be all right," Pa said. "But I always let somebody know where I'll be when I go off alone, just in case a snake throws me, or somethin'."

"Why don't we catch brumbies?" I asked. "If Mr. Parkes can make money from breaking and selling wild horses, we sure can. Ernie taught me how to trap them."

"Forget it, son. We're not that kind. Those brumbies've been around these parts longer than we have. They deserve to run free. And besides, they're too proud to be in captivity. Did any of the wild horses die when you helped Ernie round them up?"

"A few. Ernie said it was because they were run too hard."

"It isn't so. They died because they couldn't stand bein' captured and havin' their spirits broken." Pa must've seen the hurt in my eyes because he added, "I'm not against catchin' one for our own use if it's young. But it'd take too long to break a brumby to do us any good. By the time we have him all trained, it'd be winter and we'd have to turn him loose 'cause we couldn't afford winter feed." He took a bite of his biscuits and gravy. "Really good, Mary." He swallowed and winked at me across the table. "Why don't you bring your ma home a grown wombat for a house pet? I bet she'd like that."

I looked at Ma and asked, "What color would you like, Ma?"

Shocked, she stared at my deadpan face and then at Pa. Throwing her napkin on the table, she said, "Oh, you two are just alike! I don't stand a chance. Now, get out of the kitchen while I clean up!"

Pa relaxed in the rocking chair while he waited for me to finish breakfast. Ma had loaded extra food on my plate and I didn't want to see it wasted, so I kept eating. Before leaving the table, I stuck a couple of apples in my lunch sack and two strips of dried jerky. My mind was still on wild horses as I entered the sitting room.

"Where do the brumbies go in the winter, Pa?"

"In Montana, they hide in the deep canyons where the wind is blocked and the grass stays open almost all year. Around here, I'll bet it's the same. Most of the gullies and gorges will still have grass beneath the snow. The brumbies are pretty good at pawing the snow with their hooves and uncovering the range grass. I've seen it when range cows followed wild horses around like puppy dogs so they could eat what the horses pawed up. A wild horse can break a hole in the ice with his front hoof to get a drink when a cow can't." Pa paused and examined a chunk of wood he was preparing to carve.

"What's it going to be, Pa?"

"Haven't decided yet. There's somethin' hidden in there, son, just waitin' to get out. All I gotta do is figure out what it is!"

I sat on the floor and looked at the piece of wood. "Could be a horse's head," I said. "See how the grains are swirling around the nostrils?"

"That'd be grand! Maybe Moonrunner." He smiled at me and said, "The brumbies really help the station owners. I guess that's why I hate to see them captured. They aren't hurtin' anyone out there and they've saved the lives of a lot of cows and nobody knows it."

"Ernie says the brumbies cut the grass shorter than cows and it kills the grass," I said.

"That's true, son. What Ernie says is right. But wild horses also eat the old dead winter grass in the early spring. It makes it easier for the new spring grass to grow. And the shorter grass helps prevent fires from raging through the high plains and destroying all the animals and trees. It's about even when it comes to grasses, if you ask me."

"Sounds that way to me, too," I answered.

Lady whinnied loudly to remind me that she was still tied to the veranda, waiting. I leaped up and ran for the door. "I'll be home before dark. Don't worry."

Ma hurried into the sitting room, untying her apron. "Dan, saddle Girlie. I'm going to ride to the river with Casey."

"Ma! I can cross the river by myself!"

"You'll be crossing by yourself, but I'll be watching you cross to make sure you're safe, and that's all there is to it."

Pa lowered the chunk of wood he had been studying and looked up. "Mary –"

"Don't 'Mary' me! Saddle Girlie. Either I go to the river with Casey or he isn't going!"

I said, "I think it's a great idea, Ma. I'd like your company. Been a long time since we've ridden together."

Pa held a slight smile on his face as he left the room to saddle Girlie.

I really was glad to have Ma's company. We laughed and talked about silly little things, and important things, as we rode along side by side. She pointed with delight at every little bird and animal that we saw along the way. She was like a different person away from the homestead. She even looked younger. She told me that she really hated being stuck in the middle of nowhere in this strange land. It was real grown-up talk, and I felt good about it. Maybe she was trying to make me feel better and less alone, or maybe she just needed someone to talk with to make herself feel better. I don't know, but by the time we reached the Mitta Mitta about mid-morning, we felt like close friends.

The river was the lowest I'd ever seen it. I was happy about that. We let our horses drink before I started across. On the opposite side, I turned to wave. Ma waved back and yelled, "I hope you find Moonrunner. See you at home, son."

"Don't worry, Ma. I'll be home before dark. And thanks for coming with me. I really enjoyed the ride."

"Me, too! And I won't worry now," she answered. She waved and turned Girlie for home.

About noon, I reined Lady to a halt on the very spot where I had last seen Moonrunner. Lady seemed to know which way to go. She walked directly towards the hidden gorge. We followed tracks along a scrub-covered dried riverbed, working our way up a narrow gully that turned into a steep gorge less than ten feet wide. The smooth stone walls were absolutely vertical on both sides.

Eventually, the gorge widened enough to allow sunshine to reach the bottom. Directly in front of me, the gorge split into two steep channels with a narrow, rocky pedestal separating the two forks. I tied Lady to a branch, stood on the saddle and pulled myself up a woolly butt to the top of the bluff, then scooted to the very pinnacle of a large boulder where I perched like an eagle.

Standing erect, carefully balanced, I looked up the gorge. I felt like I could see to the edge of the world. This was going to be my kingdom. I stretched my arms out wide and felt the breeze on my face. "I, King Casey, am king of this gorge. You there! Curry my horse and bring me a root beer."

I removed an apple and a sandwich from my pack and sat down to eat lunch and daydream about racing Lady next Easter. Wouldn't everyone be surprised when I won?

Something moved in the brush just beyond the spring. I quickly lowered myself on top of the boulder. Ten brumbies slowly walked towards the spring, nibbling on the tender grass, totally unaware of me watching from the rocks. Just before reaching the spring, they looked back as if expecting company. Moonrunner trotted out behind the mares and nudged them several times on their flanks. The stallion sniffed the air as his mares drank from the spring. He whinnied loudly. Lady pointed her ears at the stallion and answered him. Before I could react, Moonrunner galloped across the grassy area directly towards me. Below me, Lady fought her reins, trying to break free to join the black stallion.

Moonrunner must have sensed a trap. He jammed his front hooves into the grass and abruptly stopped. He looked directly at me and whinnied shrilly. I slowly stood.

"Hello, Moonrunner. My name's Casey. Lady and I would like to be your friends. Would you like that?" Seeing me, the mares bolted for the bush. Moonrunner didn't run, but he snorted his displeasure several times. Spinning, he turned to face me again, pawing the ground angrily.

"I'm not going to hurt you, Moonrunner." I stood perfectly still.

Eventually, the stallion leaned over and snapped off some grass to show me that he wasn't afraid. Then he casually walked over to drink before joining his mares in the bush.

I didn't move for a long while after Moonrunner had disappeared.

"Moonrunner," I whispered, "you're the real King of the Gorge."

Still excited, I eased down the woolly butt and dropped the last ten feet onto the sandy riverbed. Lady was very nervous, dancing and fidgeting, still looking towards the spring.

"Easy girl, easy does it." I petted her nose and neck. "Here ya go girl, I've saved you part of my apple. Wasn't he something? How would you like to have him for a boyfriend? I'd be jealous, you know."

I untied her reins, mounted, and worked my way down the narrow gorge. After we crossed the river, Lady looked back and nickered loudly. "I know, girl. I'd like to follow him, too. But it's getting late. We've got to be home before dark. We'll come back next Sunday if you'd like." Lady must have understood because her nicker changed to a loud whinny as she broke into a fast canter towards the homestead and her new home.

★ CHAPTER NINE ★

Lady is Mine

On the days I didn't work for Ernie, I caught up on the winter woodpile and hauled stacked hay to the shed. Cutting wood had always been a chore for me and stockpiling enough wood to last the winter was major work. But I knew it was necessary and didn't complain. If the work didn't get done, our family might not survive the winter. Pa and I worked from sunup until dark every day bringing in more dead wood. Day after day, we hitched up Old Lop Ears and searched the river and gullies for drift wood or dead trees, then dragged the firewood back to the house. With me on one end of the double-action saw and Pa on the other, we sawed the trees into shorter sections, then used metal wedges to split the sections into smaller pieces for the fireplace and even smaller ones for the cook stove. It was also my job to stack the cooking wood outside the door on the back porch for Ma.

I was sawing wood with Pa one day, pulling the bucksaw back and forth, but instead of concentrating on the work I was daydreaming about some of my trips to the hidden gorge. I had learned all of Moonrunner's hiding places.

The brumbies had two secret exits out of the rugged gorge that were hidden behind boulders and brush. I had known the secret escape routes existed, but they were hard to find. Lady finally discovered one of the trails, and I outsmarted Moonrunner to find the other. I had circled around the hidden gorge and tied Lady up so she wouldn't whinny, then crept across the spur to the gorge's edge on foot. I was extremely careful not to alert the mob by stepping on dry twigs. As I peeked over the rim, the mares were grazing near the spring. Moonrunner was standing on top of a little knoll, sniffing the air, expecting company. I tossed a small rock as far as I could in the direction the stallion was looking. Instantly, Moonrunner perked his ears and tensed. He nickered to the mares. Very quietly, they moved towards the black stallion. I remained hidden and watched the horses scale the steep, rocky wall on the far side of the gorge.

The noise of the bucksaw slicing through the wood brought me back to reality. "They're not afraid of me anymore," I said to Pa.

"What?" Pa must've had no idea what I was talking about. He waited for me to pull the bucksaw across the log.

Instead of pulling, I turned loose of my end and leaned on the uncut piece of wood. "I've been around Moonrunner so many times, he's not afraid of me anymore. Once, I ate lunch right near the mares."

"That's nice, son, but if you keep daydreamin', I'll have to push and pull this saw and we'll never get done."

"Yes, sir," I said. I grabbed my end, braced myself, and gave a mighty pull to get the rhythm of the blade started again, but my eyes must have glazed over because I saw Pa shaking his head.

———— · • · ————

It was the end of my school holiday and Mr. Parkes had returned from the muster. He stood near the bunkhouse at dusk.

"Casey! I got something for you."

As I dismounted, I glanced at Ernie to see if he knew what was going on. He shrugged. I kept my eyes on Mr. Parkes' face as I led Lady across the yard, trying to judge his mood, but he held a poker face.

"You called me, sir?" I asked nervously. It was the first time I'd seen him in three weeks. He looked rugged, kind of wild.

"I understand this is your last day of work."

"Yes, sir. School starts on Monday."

Mr. Parkes handed me a piece of paper. "Here's your bill of sale. Now Lady is legally yours."

I grinned from ear to ear. "Casey Jenner" was written in bold letters across the top. A scrawled signature was at the bottom. "Thank you, sir. I really appreciate you selling her to me."

"You earned her, son. Did me a fine job. At least that's what Ernie tells me."

Ernie crossed the yard. "You bet he did. But we'd better watch out. Casey's going to enter Lady in the race next year. She'll give our horse a run for its money."

"We'd better shake hands now, Casey," Mr. Parkes said, laughing at the prospect of running against Lady. His belly shook beneath his flannel shirt as he chuckled. "If you beat me next year, I won't feel like shaking hands."

I shook his hand and answered seriously, "I understand, sir. If I had a winning record like yours, I'd be upset, too."

Ernie said, "Something tells me we'd better come up with a fast horse next year. We'll be riding against determination."

"You might be right, Ernie." Mr. Parkes adjusted his wide-brimmed hat. "Casey, stop by to see us from time to time. Maybe I'll have a paying job for you this summer."

"I'll do that, sir. Right now, I'd best get home." I swung into the saddle without using the stirrups and leaned down to shake hands with Ernie. Over the past three weeks, Ernie and I had really become good friends. "Goodbye, Ernie. Thanks for everything. I'll come see you."

It was a long ride home. When I finally arrived, I took my time feeding all the animals and gave Lady an extra helping of oats. Placing my cheek against her nose, I whispered, "You're mine, girl. Really mine." I pulled out the bill of sale. "See this piece of paper? It says I don't have to work for you anymore." I held it in front of her eyes. "That's your name right there and that's mine. That's Mr. Parkes' signature." I carefully folded the paper and put it into my shirt pocket, and whistled all the way to the house.

I wasn't prepared for the surprise awaiting me as I opened the front door. Ma had made a huge chocolate cake. They must've been listening to me doing the chores and heard me whistling across the yard because the candles were already burning.

"Ma, what's this for?" I ran to the table. "It ain't my birthday!"

"Well, in a way it is. The present you got on Easter Saturday is finally yours to keep. You worked hard to earn Lady, son." Ma had tears in her eyes. "Now, make a wish and blow out the candles before they melt and ruin the frosting."

"You must've used the whole box!" I said. The candles illuminated my face as I closed my eyes and wished everything would always be as it was at that very moment.

"Your pa and me ... well, we wanted to make it a special night, just for you, since Lady is all yours. I even fixed your favorite supper. Your pa and me are very proud of you for working like you did. Never complaining and all."

"Leave me out of this," Pa said. "It was all your ma's idea. I had nothin' to do with it."

"That's why you made a special trip into Omeo to buy

the chocolate and the root beer!"

Pa waited for me to blow out the candles before sitting down. Ma lifted the cake aside and placed a meat pie on the table.

"With cornbread?" I asked.

Ma nodded happily.

"And butter?"

"Churned some while your pa was in Omeo." She removed the hot cornbread from the oven and sat down.

"I'm glad I went to Omeo today, 'cause when I stopped by the courthouse to check on the details of owning this property, I ran into an old digger that knew my daddy," Pa said as he cut me a big slice of cornbread and handed it across the table.

"What'd he say, Pa?" I slapped on a dab of butter.

"He said that Daddy and his partner arrived from San Francisco halfway through the Omeo gold run, around 1855 or '56, he couldn't be sure. This digger –"

"What's his name?" Ma asked.

"Jamison, I think he said it was. Anyway, this digger had a claim on Dry Gully Creek next to Daddy and his partner. He said that Omeo was a lawless town back then. Killin's, no sheriff. The Dry Gully claim didn't show any color, so Daddy and his partner worked their way up Livingston Creek and finally found flakes of gold on this place."

"Here?" I was astounded. "That's why the old sluice box is down by the dry creek."

Pa nodded. "Then, in the fall of 1858, Daddy's partner was killed in a knife fight for salting their old claim on Dry Gully Creek."

"What's salting mean, Pa?" I asked.

"It's when a miner sprinkles a little gold dust around to make it look as if the claim is worth somethin'. Apparently, it wasn't worth a plug nickel, so Daddy's partner was killed."

"Did Grandpa help salt the mine?" I asked. "The digger didn't think so. But because Daddy was a partner in the claim, both were blamed for the salting."

"Then Grandpa isn't a crook."

"It doesn't seem so. But this Jamison liked my daddy. Keep in mind, son, it was different back then. Really wild."

"I've heard that a lot of the settlers were convicts from England and Ireland," Ma said. "Whether your grandpa was a crook or not, we can't change the past. We are who we are: good, honest, law-abiding people."

Pa nodded and went on. "When the Omeo gold run ended in 1860, Daddy continued workin' the claim out back. He had diverted the spring to supply water for his sluice. Eventually, Daddy earned enough with his findin's and trappin' to finally get a little money ahead. Jamison said that when the Land Act of 1860 became law, Daddy selected this 320 acres, and built this house. He was goin' to send for me and my ma."

Ma touched Pa's arm. "I'm so happy for you."

I'd never seen tears in Pa's eyes before. I stopped eating

and looked across the table as he wiped his eyes.

"Me, too, Pa," I said. "Did he send for you?"

"Nah, he didn't. Gold was discovered in Cassilis, about 15 miles southeast of Omeo. Not wanting to miss out again, my daddy rushed to Cassilis to stake a new claim, but ended up workin' for someone else on a gold dredge the rest of his life. Jamison said that he used to stop by here about twice a month to have a drink of whisky with my daddy. He said that Daddy really worked hard to build up this place. And he was goin' to send for us, 'cause in 1890, Jamison helped Daddy write a letter home and Daddy deposited enough funds in the Omeo bank for us to reach Melbourne." Pa looked down at his hands, unable to speak for a moment. He glanced at Ma and tried to smile.

"The digger was visitin' Daddy when he died. He said that Daddy was feedin' Hoppy and just rolled off the veranda. He died never seein' me as a grown man. And he never knew that I had married the most beautiful woman in the whole United States, and that he had a marvelous grandson named Casey. It was Jamison that buried Daddy beneath the blue gum tree and carved those words on the hardwood plank stickin' out of Daddy's grave."

Ma squeezed my hand, and reached to hold Pa's hand at the same time. I'd never felt so close to my ma and pa in my entire life.

Ma said, "He sent for his family at the end and never gave up loving you both. He might not have found much gold here, but I think the real gold was in his heart."

Pa nodded but didn't say anything. I could tell he was all choked up inside and I wanted to make him smile. That's why I said, "I'm ready for some of that cake."

———·•·———

By Sunday I was really worried about returning to school, too worried to enjoy seeing Moonrunner again. So I stayed in the shed all day, currying Lady and shining her hooves, playing with Hoppy and polishing the old saddle till it looked almost new.

"They can't laugh at me now," I whispered as I combed Lady's tail for the tenth time. "You're beautiful, girl." Lady nickered.

After lying awake worrying half the night, on Monday morning I overslept and had to put Lady into a fast canter over the hill to arrive just before the bell rang. Lady fancy-stepped across the schoolyard with her four white stockings shining in the morning sun. I was really proud of her. It was like riding in a parade. I glanced around and saw Mike and Jimmy watching me, but they said nothing.

Lady nickered at me when I turned her loose in the yard. "Take it easy, girl. Nothing to be afraid of. I'll see you at recess." I glanced at the other horses milling about in the yard. "It's a shame to put such a beautiful horse in the same yard with such ugly nags!" I held out my apple for her to eat and entered the schoolhouse just as the bell rattled my tired brain.

During the morning, I yawned and yearned for recess. All I could think about was Lady. When it finally arrived, I ran out to check on her and heard snickering behind me.

"Hey, cheater! Your big mouth really got us in trouble." It was Mike. "My father says your grandfather was a cheat. You're just like him."

All three sang,

> "Sam Jenner, gobbledygook.
> Cheater, rat, crook.
> Casey Jenner, clinkety-clank.
> Cheater, rat, Yank."

"Your Pa's grandfather was a convict!" I said angrily, still petting Lady.

"But he never cheated anyone in Australia," Mike answered. "There's a difference."

"There's no difference," I shouted. "A crook's a crook!"

"I see your mummy bought you new school clothes," Charlie said.

"Look at his baggy pants!" Jimmy said.

"Did you bring another baseball bat, Cheater Yank?" Mike asked. "We need some firewood."

"Did you see that old nag he rode to school?" Jimmy teased.

Mike laughed loudly. "He should've stuck to the mule!" All of them laughed.

"Doesn't look like there's any difference between the mule he rode to school before the muster and the mule he rode this morning," Charlie said.

I stopped petting Lady and turned to face the gang. I wasn't smiling. I'd had enough teasing. There were only three of them. Frank had remained on the school steps, alone.

"You ain't supposed to be bothering me," I said. I was weighing my chances if I had to fight. Jimmy didn't count, he was too little. I would be fighting Mike and Charlie at the same time. My ears burned and my stomach heaved. I was determined to not let their words rip away my new-found confidence. Whether my grandpa was a crook or not didn't matter. This was about me. But I knew that, as much as I wanted to at that moment, fighting the gang wasn't the answer. I had to walk away, like Miss Evans said. I had to think of something better than fighting, something that would really humiliate them.

"Isn't that the old donkey that finished last at the Omeo Rodeo?" Charlie said.

"Nah, it couldn't be. Nobody would be seen riding that old nag," Mike answered.

"Except crooked Casey Jenner!" All three boys roared with laughter.

The recess bell rang. It was over. I had made it through without fighting. As I turned to have a last look at Lady before going inside, an idea formed. I knew, eventually, the time would come.

After a few weeks, Frank and I were on better terms. I could tell that he wanted to be my friend, but it was difficult forgetting him sitting on my arm while Mike kicked me in the head. The others went about their normal business of pulling the girls' hair and dipping their braids in the inkwell, throwing spit wads in the classroom when Miss Evans wasn't looking and taunting me whenever they had the chance. I decided it was time. I wrote a note while Miss Evans was reading aloud and passed it around the room.

Mike, Frank, Charlie, Jimmy

Meet me at the Forks after school, today. We'll race to the Anderson place. The losers must curry the winner's horse during recess for a week, in front of the whole school.

Casey Jenner

My stomach was in knots the rest of the day. Out of the corner of my eye, I watched the note being secretly passed from desk to desk. It was a bold challenge. The gang had to accept or lose face. This was it! Could Lady run? Was she as fast as Ernie said? I was about to find out.

★ CHAPTER TEN ★

Racing the Gang

Every kid in school turned out for the race. Miss Evans even arrived in her buggy. A few kids had ridden ahead to the finish line. The rest were mounted, intent on riding behind to watch. The gang was surprisingly quiet. They weren't teasing me now. Instead they were talking to their horses. It would be embarrassing for them if I actually won the race and they had to curry Lady for a week.

Lady danced around in tight circles and nickered lightly.

"This is it, girl. You know it, don't you?" I leaned over the saddle and patted her soft neck. She twitched her ears in recognition.

"Ya ready, Jenner?" Mike said.

I answered, "Who's going to start us?"

"It's your race, at least before it starts. You pick someone."

I walked Lady over to where Miss Evans was sitting in her buggy. "Will you start us?"

"Of course, Casey, I'd be glad to. And good luck."

Miss Evans stepped from her buggy. "Are you boys ready?"

They all nodded, looking down the road towards the finish line.

"To my understanding, the Anderson's place is the finish line, and the losers must curry the winner's horse for a week. Is that right?"

Again, the gang agreed. I wondered how she had learned about my challenge.

"Take your positions." She waited a moment. "Get ready … get set … go!"

All five horses lunged forward. Mike and Charlie squeezed their horses together and knocked Lady off stride. Lady spun around, confused. She was twenty feet behind and the race had barely started.

With desperation in my voice, I leaned over the saddle and whispered, "Come on, Lady. We've got to catch them!" Near panic, I reined Lady down the road and slapped her with the tips of the leather reins. I pleaded, "Lady, you've got to run. You can do it. Don't let them beat us!"

Lady seemed to understand. She suddenly came alive, chasing the dust of the other four horses. Her stride became longer as she gained momentum. At the quarter point, the horses were strung out down the long dirt road in single file with Lady in the rear. I remembered what Ernie had said: *If you ever want her to run, give Lady her head.* I leaned forward in the saddle and let the reins go slack. "Go get 'em, Lady!"

She understood. Suddenly she wasn't the same gentle little mare I had ridden all holiday. It was like riding the north wind itself. I passed Jimmy. Lady was running faster and faster. It seemed to me her strides were so long that she only touched ground every twenty feet. Even then she only touched it lightly, as though she was just making sure it was still beneath her.

I passed Charlie, who was madly yelling at his horse to run faster. The wind whipped around my head, making my eyes water and my ears hurt. All I could do was hang on. Lady leaped by Frank's big chestnut and was still picking up speed. Her stride was faster than a gallop. She was like an antelope flying across the open desert, with her belly low to the ground, stretching for the next step, floating in the air between hoof beats.

Mike glanced back to see Lady and me right on his tail. He frantically whipped his horse. For several hundred feet, it was neck and neck. I felt Lady's hooves hitting the ground in long rhythmic beats. I felt my own heart pounding in my head. I felt the quiet power of Lady beneath me.

In two more leaps, Lady was in front. When she crossed the finish line, she was ahead by two full lengths.

"We won, Lady! We won!" I shouted. Lady didn't slow

down. Just as Ernie said, there was no stopping her once she got started. I let her run up the hill towards home. Finally, she heard my calming voice and slowed to a fast canter at the top. It was over. We had won.

As we approached the house, Lady was breathing easy and my heart had returned to normal.

"Yahoo! Ma! Pa! We did it. You should have seen Lady run!"

Ma hurried onto the veranda. "What is it, Casey? Are you hurt?"

"We won, Ma. We raced them all and we won!"

"Raced who?" Ma asked, getting swept up in my excitement.

"The gang at school. I challenged them all and we won!"

Pa arrived from the shed. "Pa! We raced them all at school, me and Lady. Beat them by a mile!"

Pa scraped a handful of white lather from Lady's neck and chest. "That's great, son, but you'd better rub her down right away. And keep her away from the water. It might give her the colic."

My enthusiasm was crushed. I slid from the saddle and dejectedly walked towards the shed, leading Lady.

I heard Ma say, "That was awfully mean, Dan. Let him have a little fun. You stepped on his excitement and squashed it flatter'n a June bug!"

"You're right. I was just worried about the horse. Casey! Wait up."

I was rubbing Lady down with the hessian bag when Pa entered the shed.

"Where'd you race, son?"

"From the forks near the school along the creek to the Anderson place."

"That's about a mile and a half," he commented.

"That's why I picked it. Ernie said she was a long distance runner," I said, rubbing without looking up.

"You challenged 'em?"

"Yes, sir. I had to know if she could run or not."

"How'd she run?" Pa asked.

I suddenly whirled around, unable to control my feelings. "We won, Pa! We won hands down. We were a long way back in the beginning, but I remembered Ernie told me to let Lady find her own stride. From then on, it was our race."

"It's a nice feelin' havin' the fastest horse in school," Pa said.

"It sure is," I answered. "After ridin' Old Lop Ears for so long."

"It could hurt your chances to win next year."

"Why's that?" I asked.

"The boys'll all tell their parents. Pretty soon, everyone in the territory will know how fast Lady can run. They'll find faster horses."

"I hadn't thought about that. It's just the gang was teasing me something awful about Grandpa being a crook and they called Lady a mule. I just had to do something!"

"I know how you feel. Sometimes, though, it's best to keep your pride to yourself. Lasts you longer that way."

"I kind of knew she could do it. I guess I didn't have to prove it."

"Well, we can't change it now. But it's like how I always beat you in checkers. I don't go braggin' about it, do I?"

"You don't always beat me!" I flared.

"That's why I don't brag about it!" Pa laughed.

"I'll walk Lady around until she cools down. Get the checkerboard out and we'll see who wins," I laughed.

"That sounds like another challenge to me."

"The way I feel now, you don't stand a chance."

———————

In the morning, just before recess, I raised my hand in class. "Miss Evans?"

"What is it, Casey?"

"I'd like to say somethin', Ma'am."

"Someth*ing*, not someth*in'*, and you have the floor," she answered.

"Yes, Ma'am." I slowly stood and looked at the sullen-faced gang I had beaten yesterday. Frank had congratulated me, but the other three hadn't said a word all morning.

"Well, Casey. If you have something to say," she emphasized the word *something*, "please say it."

"Ma'am, I'd like to take back the bet on the race I made yesterday. I knew Lady could outrun the other horses. The losers don't have to curry my horse for a week, if they don't want to." I quickly sat down and stared at my hands on the desk in front of me.

"If that's what you want, Casey." She turned to the class. "It's time for recess, everyone outside."

The classroom sounded like a hornet's nest as the excited kids left the building. Why had I backed down? I had won the race and had every right to get revenge on the teasing gang.

"Casey," Miss Evans stopped me as I stood to leave. "That was a very grown-up thing you just did."

I hurried out the door and spotted Mike sitting alone against the large gum tree where I usually sat. He looked terrible. I suddenly felt sorry for him. His Pa must've beaten the living daylight out of him last night. Charlie and Jimmy were kicking a ball back and forth with some other kids. Jimmy was limping.

Mike didn't see me until I sat down beside him. He had a lost look in his eyes, as if he'd just given up on life.

"You're sittin' in my place," I said.

Mike nodded.

"Ya know, Mike, I think I could whip you good in a real fight, just between you and me."

Mike looked amazed. "You're a tough nut, Casey Jenner." There was a long silence. Then he leaped to his feet and screamed, "Get out of my life! I hate you! Go back to America."

★ CHAPTER ELEVEN ★

First Winter

Frost lingered on the ground and crunched beneath my feet each morning.

A few weeks after my race with the gang, I finished my Saturday morning chores while Pa was milking Bossie, changed the hay in Hoppy's bed and, since the weather looked promising, decided to take Lady out for a ride. The high plains above our house had already had a couple of snowstorms, and I knew they were a prelude to an early winter. This could be my last chance to have a look around.

Lady nickered when I stepped from the veranda. "Want to go riding, Lady?" She nickered again and whinnied loudly as she pranced once around the yard before returning to impatiently wait for me to open the gate. I led her to the shed and saddled her. Pa was there, staring at the hayloft. He was leaning on the pitchfork with the same worried look I had seen the night I brought Lady home.

"Look at that." Pa pointed upward.

"Is it a possum?"

Pa shook his head. "We don't have as much hay as I'd hoped we'd have for winter. The land was lyin' fallow too long. Your grandpa never worked the bottoms."

"Wasn't Grandpa a farmer in Kentucky before he ran off to California?" I asked.

"The farm belonged to my ma. My daddy hated farmin'. That's why he skedaddled to California when I was born. I saw him only once after that. He came all the way back to Kentucky just to say goodbye. I was about six years old. All I remember is a man that smelled like tobacco and had stains on his bushy beard. His teeth were brown. His hands were cracked and sunburned. He stayed for a short time and got bored. Gold was in his blood. Your grandpa was a digger, not a farmer. He never liked the cold either. "Goin' to find gold in Australia," I remember him sayin'. "When I strike the yella stuff I'll send for you and your ma." Never heard from him again, not even a single letter. Until we got word that he'd died four years ago." Pa chuckled sadly. "I wonder if Mount Sam is named after my pa."

"We'll manage, Pa. We always do," I said. "Next spring, we'll get a good start on the land."

"But that's next spring. What are we goin' to do this

winter? I feel bad. We didn't get the bottomland plowed in time."

"We didn't arrive until Christmas, Pa. It was mid-summer here. We worked hard and did all we could. We got the kitchen garden planted," I added, "and the ditches cleaned out from the spring, and the cistern mucked out and a new hole dug for the outhouse. And saved the fruit trees from dying."

"I know, we worked hard, but – come here, son. Let's talk about this."

I clutched Lady's reins, feeling something bad was about to happen. Pa looked at me. I could see that he was trying to choose the right words.

Finally he said, "When we got Lady in April, I thought we'd have enough hay. We didn't make it, son. Look for yourself. The hay should be touchin' the rafters."

I felt a cold knot forming in my stomach. The hay was three feet below the rafters. "We can ration the hay, make it last. Or buy extra hay in Omeo."

"We don't have money to buy hay. We barely have enough left for groceries. That's why your ma's been cannin' so hard. Do you remember when we talked about the brumbies winterin' in the deep gorges?"

I remembered, but chose not to answer. Tightening my jaw, I waited for what I knew was coming next.

"I'm afraid Lady's goin' to have to winter with the brumbies. There's barely enough hay to feed the work animals."

"Lady's a work animal now. She takes me to school. Why can't we turn out Girlie or Lop Ears?"

"You already know the answer to that question, son. Girlie's too old to be accepted by the brumbies. And she's the only horse we have to pull the bullock wagon. And Old Lop Ears is a mule."

Heat boiled in my stomach. My brain was about to blow off my ears. Losing Lady would be too much for me to handle and I knew it.

"She'll die, Pa! Lady'll die and you'll have killed her! You sold Arrowhead out from under me and now you're going to kill Lady." I leaped into the saddle, spun my horse around violently and galloped out of the shed with tears stinging my eyes.

"We'll run away, Lady, and never come back. Pa can't take you away from me! We'll show him!"

I raced up the mountain, yearning to be alone with Lady. Only she could understand how I felt. How could Pa be so heartless?

It was freezing at the top of the mountain. I didn't have my coat. Tying up Lady, I crawled into a small cave obscured by a weird looking pile of rocks. It was like a private hideout, a world that no one knew about except me. I watched the lights far below blink out one by one until the entire valley was pitch black. The Southern Cross was now my only companion. Eventually, when it became too cold to sit still, I carefully worked my way down the mountain and returned to the ranch just before midnight.

Pa was sitting by the fire, whittling, as I crossed the sitting room to warm my hands. My cheeks felt like cold porcelain, my lips were numb. I had been riding and sitting all day. I waited for my shivering to stop and looked at Pa's face. He hadn't said a word. He was staring into the fire. A half-burned log snapped loudly, startling me.

"I'm sorry for what I said, Pa."

"That's okay, Casey. I know you didn't mean it."

"When would it be best to turn her loose?"

"Soon. A bad storm could hit at any time. The brumbies must accept her before winter."

"Guess I'll ride Old Lop Ears to school again."

Pa nodded. "Where you plannin' on turnin' her loose? With Moonrunner?"

"Yeah. He trusts me. And there's a hidden gorge where he runs. It'll be easier to capture her there in the spring."

"When would you like to turn her loose?"

"Next week, I guess," I answered, still gazing into the fire.

"Next week might be too late, son. There's change a-comin'. We've already had two snows."

"That's the way it has to be, Pa. It's goin' to kill me to let her go after sharin' so much." Tears fell from my eyes and ran down my cheeks. "I love her more than anything, Pa."

"I know, son. It's painful. Every chance we get, we'll ride out and check on her, just to see how she's doin'."

"I'd like that, Pa."

"Your ma left supper on the table before she went to bed. You'd better eat it or you'll have the same thing for breakfast!"

It was a long week. I had a hard time concentrating at school and could barely sleep at night. Instead I sat at the window talking with Lady. What would I do if Lady died? How could I do anything ever again without Lady?

To my surprise, the kids at school didn't laugh when I told them I had to ride Old Lop Ears again. Instead, Maggie and Mary told me how sorry they were and offered to help find Moonrunner when I released Lady on Sunday. Frank wanted to come too. Even little Gracie wanted to help. But I insisted that it was something I had to do alone. In my heart, though, I doubted if I would be strong enough to let her go.

Early Sunday morning, I rode Lady bareback down Bingo Munjie Creek towards the Mitta Mitta River. I had curried Lady and given her an extra helping of oats to send her on her way. Old Lop Ears plodded along behind, being led on a short rope with my saddle on his back. The cinch was barely long enough to stretch around the mule's stomach. I was filled with dread and extremely concerned. What if Moonrunner rejected Lady? How could she survive? I wouldn't be around to help her if she got into trouble. I looked over my shoulder at the mule and shook my head. "I'd rather walk than ride you to school again."

The day promised to be very cold and windy. A line of dark brown clouds was on the horizon, rolling over Mount

Sam like a blanket. A fresh breeze rippled the surface of the Mitta Mitta. As the wind intensified, it ripped leaves from the blue gums and woolly butts along the edge of the water.

"Better hurry," I said to Lady. "Don't want to get caught in a blizzard."

The sound of the howling wind was cut off the moment I crossed the river and turned into thick brush that led into the hidden gorge.

"This is going to be a nice place to winter, Lady. Looks like plenty of grass around. It's nicer than the shed. You should be right comfortable." My words comforted me, but I felt like a traitor. I walked Lady slowly up the gorge to the spring. She had no idea what was happening.

"Don't see any tracks, Lady girl." At the head of the gorge, I stopped. I hadn't seen any sign of Moonrunner or his mares. "Lady, he's got to be here somewhere." I became very worried. "Let's find him, girl."

Lady picked her way up a narrow trail at the head of the gorge. On top, the wind had increased to a loud howl, blowing furiously across the spur. My sheepskin coat stopped most of the cold but there was no stopping the wind from seeping through the buttonholes and up my back as I leaned over Lady for warmth. I couldn't feel the reins in my right hand. My left hand was jammed into my coat pocket, squeezing a single lump of sugar for Lady.

"The wind's really whippin'! Let's get a move on, Lady. I ain't leavin' you here by yourself." I tried to put Lady into a fast canter but Old Lop Ears refused to run. At the next gorge, I quickly dropped over the rim into shelter. We walked down the gorge to the Mitta Mitta, but still saw no sign of the brumbies. I turned south, directly into the wind. "Let's go home, girl. We'll try again next week."

The ugly brown clouds turned to fierce black as I leaned forward and covered my eyes. Sleet, driven ahead of the snow, blew harshly on my face. As I neared the mouth of the hidden gorge, I decided to take shelter rather than be caught on the open river in the blizzard.

"Whoa, Lady." I jumped from her back and tied my red handkerchief to a tree limb near the trail. "Just in case. Don't know how bad it's going to be, Lady. I want Pa to know where I am." I mounted and turned up the gully.

I tied both animals to an old tree next to a sandy inlet near the spring. The snow was already sticking to the opposite rim of the gorge. Gathering firewood, I dug through my pockets for matches. I hadn't brought any, so I huddled into a tight ball at Lady's feet and tried to doze. It was going to be a long, uncomfortable wait for the storm to pass.

The ground vibrated with hoof beats. I ran from the inlet just in time to see the last of the mares gallop by. Moonrunner appeared through the mist of falling snow. I was so captivated by the stallion's splendor and beauty that the brumbies were out of sight before I reacted.

"He's here, Lady. Moonrunner's here. Let's go!" I removed Lady's bridle, looped a rope around her neck and patted the mule. "I'll be right back, Lop Ears."

I walked Lady quietly towards the spring. The wind, howling overhead, muffled the sound of Lady's steps as we moved like phantoms through the wind-whipped blizzard.

Moonrunner warily watched us approach. I stopped, holding Lady close to me. I handed her the sugar. "This is to remember me by, girl. Don't forget old Case. I'll be back in the spring to fetch you."

As Lady munched the sugar, I stood face to face with the black stallion. He pawed the ground angrily, spun around and lowered his ears, feigning a charge. My throat was dry. I had never been this close to Moonrunner. I didn't feel the cold, but shivers passed through my body.

"Easy boy. I'm not going to hurt you. Easy does it. This is Casey. You remember me, don't you? I want you to take care of Lady for me. Can you do that for old Casey?" Without taking my eyes from Moonrunner, I slipped the rope from Lady and patted her flank. "Go on, girl. This'll be your home for a while."

Lady stood beside me. She whinnied loudly. Moonrunner whinnied louder, his lips curled back, showing his teeth. Lady tossed her head and took several steps forward. Her ears perked. She nickered quietly. Moonrunner whinnied again. Lady slowly approached the stallion. For a full minute, they stood nose to nose, smelling each other. Suddenly, the stallion wheeled and trotted towards his mares. Lady trotted off beside him. I stood alone in the snow and watched.

The wailing wind above echoed in my ears as I turned around and walked down the gorge.

"I love you, girl," I whispered. "I'm sorry we can't feed you. I won't sleep all winter worrying about you. Please understand. Please, please don't hate me for not being able to take care of you." My heart felt like it had swollen to the size of my head and tears flowed from my eyes. But all the tears in the world wouldn't erase the fact that I had failed Lady, just as I had failed Arrowhead.

When I got back to the inlet, Old Lop Ears looked at me with doleful eyes, patiently waiting to go home. "You ain't much company, you dang-burned mule. Weren't for you eatin' Lady's food, I wouldn't have to turn her loose." Suddenly angry and frustrated, I doubled my fists and charged the mule. "I hate you! I hate you!" I hit the mule as hard as I could with both fists.

Lop Ears leaped sideways, snapping the branch I had tied him to. He spun around and trotted down the canyon, braying angrily as he disappeared into the blizzard.

"Go on, leave me!" I yelled, shaking my fist in the air. "I hope you die in the storm!" I slowly lowered my hand into my pocket and stood in the gorge for a long time with the sound of the storm raging above me.

The storm intensified. Cold wind swirled down the face of the gorge. It was going to be a terrible storm.

I was in serious trouble and I knew it. The storm might last for days. I had forgotten to bring emergency matches. I

couldn't light a fire. I had to get home. But wading the Mitta
Mitta in a blizzard wasn't an option. I felt half frozen already.
Convulsive shivers rattled my body. My teeth ached from
chattering. I started walking. I had to. I trudged down the
gorge clutching the sheepskin coat tightly around my ears.
Untying my red bandana from the tree, I knotted it tightly
around my neck.

Near the Mitta Mitta River, I heard Old Lop Ears bray. I
could barely see him through the blowing snow. The faithful
old mule was waiting to carry me across the river! Running
to grab his reins, I petted the mule's face. "I'm sorry, Lop
Ears. I'll never be mad at you again!" The mule let me mount
him, but I couldn't see the river. I couldn't see anything. I had
to depend on the mule. "Let's go home, Lop Ears. There's a
warm shed waiting for you, and a bucket full of oats."

I put my head down on the mule's neck and closed my
eyes. The mule plodded through the storm. Several times, I
looked up to see where we were, but all I saw was snow. After
a while, I stopped looking. I just clung to the mule's neck,
balanced myself in the saddle, and prayed my misery would
soon end.

Suddenly it was dark and quiet. The wind had stopped.
I whispered, "Keep movin' Lop Ears!" but the mule refused
to move. I sat up slowly and opened my eyes. We were in the
shed. We were home! Sliding down, I fell on my face. My
legs wouldn't move. I was too stiff from the cold to walk. I
managed to crawl across the hay to Lady's oat bucket. Looking

at her stall, I was filled with anguish. Warm tears trickled down my frozen face. I pulled myself into a sitting position and managed to scoot the bucket towards the mule.

I knew a warm fire awaited me inside the house, but I couldn't stand. I kept rubbing and slapping my legs to get them warm. I managed to pull Lady's saddle blanket down on top of me. All I could think of was my misery and heartache. "Please, God!" I whispered. "Don't let anything happen to her."

Lady's survival through the winter depended on Moonrunner. I tried to picture Lady standing beside the black stallion in some warm gorge, out of the wind. I dragged more hay around myself, curled up beneath Lady's blanket, and cried until my heart felt as if it had burst open.

CHAPTER TWELVE

The Trap Line

The storm continued for three days before it finally passed beyond the Snowy Mountains into New South Wales. When it was over, my entire world consisted of just two colors: the piercing white of the snow, so bright that it hurt my eyes, and the brilliant blue of the sky, so intense that it didn't seem real. Snow draped heavily on sagging branches around the house. Icicles as thick as my wrist hung along the edge of the veranda.

I had cleaned and re-cleaned the traps so many times during the storm that the rusty black metal was now shiny blue-grey. Pa taught me how to set a trap without catching my fingers. I'd practiced in front of the fireplace, snapping the trap closed with the kitchen broom. And I'd cleaned and oiled the old Winchester rifle several times to make sure it was in good shape.

But I was beginning to have doubts about trapping. I knew that trapping was the only way for me to earn money for Lady, yet my heart was telling me to hang the traps back in the shed. Grandpa had trapped; Pa had trapped when he was my age, so what was wrong with me? I'd killed rabbits for us to eat. But trapping animals, causing them so much pain, was somehow different. Last night I had a terrible dream about being caught in a huge trap. But I couldn't talk with my parents about it. Ma and Pa had been too excited about me carrying on a family tradition. So I kept quiet and cleaned the traps as if nothing was wrong.

The bright morning sun burst into my room. I dressed warmly and had the traps dangling from a rafter on the front veranda by the time Ma had hot porridge, biscuits and ham gravy on the table. After eating my breakfast as slowly as I could, I fetched my homemade snowshoes and sheepskin gloves from my room.

By that time, Pa was up. He was more excited than I was about trapping. He set his coffee cup on the mantel and removed the Winchester from its cradle. Checking to make sure it was loaded, he placed it carefully on the mantel beside his cup. "Goin' to set the trap line along Bingo Munjie like we talked about?"

"Yep," I answered quickly, not wanting to get tied up in a long conversation. "The first one will be just down from the bridge." I laced my boots tighter than usual so my foot wouldn't slip.

"Think you got the knack of settin' the traps with gloves on?"

"Practiced all week," I answered.

"And broke off the broom handle twice. Now I have to sweep the floor sitting down," Ma yelled from the kitchen.

I smiled at Pa, put on my coat, slung the rifle over my shoulder and stepped outside. It was extremely cold and still. I knocked a couple of icicles loose with the butt of the rifle so I could see the shed. Hoppy peered through the shed window, curious about the noise. I smiled and called out, "Hello Hoppy! Have a good sleep?"

Pa stepped outside and bent down to help me strap on my snowshoes. "How does that feel?"

The snowshoe flopped on my foot. "Good. Seems tight enough."

"See you tonight, son. Be extra careful. The drifts along the edge of the creek are dangerous. New snow gets a little tricky, sometimes."

Hoisting the traps over my shoulder, I stepped awkwardly through a snowdrift that had curled around the house and piled high near the veranda. Hoppy had returned to her warm bed. I didn't blame her. It was going to be a miserable day. Filled with trepidation, I waved to Pa and trudged down the hill towards the creek. The brilliant sunlight bouncing off the white snow sent pain shooting deep into my squinting eyes. It had been much easier setting traps by the fireplace than in the freezing snow. The traps sank into the soft snow when I opened the jaws to set the trigger. The best way was to sit on top of the snow and bend the trap open over my knee. My bottom got wet and cold. I was miserable long before I had the first trap set and anchored to a tree.

Determined to do better and not be a disappointment to Pa, I continued plowing through the soft, powdery snow carrying the remaining eleven traps, their chains slapping against my legs, and the Winchester rifle slung over my shoulder. The creek was totally hidden, running silently beneath the snow. An animal scurried away, startling me. Floating silently in the stark blue sky, a lone black cockatoo, searching for something to eat, weaved between trees that looked like frozen giants.

The next trap was set in half the time. By evening, just as the pale sun went down behind Mount Hotham, I completed the trap line and turned for home. I reached the veranda after dark, clumsily removed my snowshoes and stood them against the wall. Brushing the snow from my damp, frozen pants, I entered the sitting room.

Ma looked up from the ham and beans she was cooking and smiled. "How'd it go, son?"

"Took longer than expected, but I got them all set."

"You look frozen."

"I feel frozen. That food sure smells good. It warms my insides!" I stood in front of the fireplace, holding my hands together to capture the warmth of the fire.

"Where's the end of the line?" Pa asked. Smoke curled upwards from his pipe and lingered in thin layers against the rafters before drifting out the cracked window. The kerosene lantern, hanging in the middle of the sitting room, was turned down to half-wick.

"Near the Mitta Mitta, where the creek dumps into the river."

"You made it all the way to the Mitta Mitta? You did good!"

"Glad to be home." I removed my wet boots and coat and hung them on a hook beside the front door. I unloaded the rifle, wiped it dry and hung it above the mantel.

"Hot bread's almost ready," Ma said. "You must be hungry."

"Totally starved is more like it," I answered as I sat down at the table. "I'm so cold inside I think my stomach's froze solid."

"Frozen solid," Ma said.

When Pa joined me at the table, I asked, "How often should I run the line?"

"Three or four times a week. With you not gettin' home from school until dark, that's hard. I figure if you run it early Saturday mornin', then again on Sunday afternoon, I'll run the line mid-week."

"You shouldn't have to do my work, Pa. Best I stay home one day, don't you think?"

"No, I don't think!" Ma answered as she placed some

freshly baked bread on the table. "You've missed enough school, with the blizzard and all. If you have to miss more because of the trap line, we'll put the traps back in the shed. And that's the end of that!"

"Your ma's right, son. Anyway, settin' the traps was the hard part."

"How you goin' to find where I set the traps?" I asked.

Ma touched my arm. Her touch felt like a feather landing on my wrist. "Son, this is a new country and a new start. You're going to learn to speak better English. You must say, 'going to find,' not 'goin' to find'."

"But I talk like Pa."

"Listen to your mother, Casey. I'm too old to change. Start speakin' good like she says."

"You're going to improve your English and that's all there is to it," Ma said. "I'm going to write a letter to Miss Evans asking her not to allow you to get away with any English mistakes."

"Yes, Ma'am. I'll work on it." I didn't see anything wrong with Pa's English. I turned to him and smiled, but he held a stern look in his eye. For Ma's sake, I said, "How are you *going* to find where I set the traps?"

Pa's eyes smiled as he sipped his coffee. "That's better. We're *going* to wait until next Saturday before we run the line. The traps'll lose our human smell by then."

"Pass the honey," I said. "What do you think I'll trap?" I spread butter on my hot bread and dropped on a blob of blue-gum honey.

"I don't really know. They don't have coyotes, wolverines or minks here. No tellin'– *telling* – what you'll catch. Your grandpa trapped possums. The red fox's hide used to be worth somethin', I was told, but there's so many of them around these parts, they ain't worth much. A silver fox was the thing to catch in Montana."

"How much would a silver fox bring?" I asked.

"A hundred dollars, sometimes. Dependin' if it was late caught or not."

"A hundred dollars! For one pelt? Wow!"

"They're pretty rare. I held a silver pelt in my hands once in Biddle. It was really somethin'."

"I wish I was trappin' in Montana," I said. Realizing I had used bad English, I waited for Ma to correct me.

"Trapping," she said.

"Trapping," I repeated. "What do you guess a silver possum would sell for?"

Pa laughed. "Is there such a thing?"

"I don't know. I'll ask my friends at school."

Ma said, "Those pesky possums are pretty common along the creek, just like the red fox. Hides can't be worth a plug nickel."

"What about koalas? They have nice furs," I asked.

Ma said, "I saw a golden possum in Omeo at the rodeo. It was alive, raised from a baby by an old digger. Kept him from going crazy from loneliness, he told me."

"What would the hide be worth?" I asked.

"Lots, I imagine," Pa answered.

"I'm going to catch one," I said, becoming more enthusiastic about trapping. "Then I'll have enough money to feed Lady so she won't have to spend the winter with the brumbies. I'll buy her a new saddle with real silver and a fancy bridle and a diamond-woven saddle blanket like the one I saw at the Omeo Rodeo."

The countryside was totally white when Pa and I left the protection of the veranda early Saturday morning. I wanted to go check on Lady but Pa said we had to run the trap line. It hadn't snowed since the blizzard, but the freezing weather had kept the snow from melting.

Ma stood in the sunshine. She handed Pa the rifle and said, "Don't bring any rabbits home unless they're already trapped. Seems like one more rabbit stew and I'll hate the taste of rabbit for the rest of my life."

Snowshoeing on top of the frozen snow was much easier than plowing through new snow. The cold air hurt my lungs. I kept my mouth shut and breathed slowly through my nose. Ice had frozen around my nostrils. At the first trap, we found fox tracks, but the trap itself was empty.

"Let's move the trap a little and hide it under the snow," Pa said. The next three traps were as empty as the first. As we approached the fifth, I saw grayish-white fur and rushed ahead, only to find the remains of a rabbit.

Pa came up behind me. "Somethin' beat you to it," he said. He bent down to study the tracks around the trap. "It was a dingo or a dog. Too big to be a fox. Leave the rabbit where it is and reset the trap a few feet away. Maybe when whatever it was comes back to finish his dinner, we can surprise him."

I stared at the dead rabbit. Poor animal! It must've really suffered! I thought. I wished that I had never set the trap.

Pa misunderstood the look on my face. "You can't expect to have all your traps full on the first day. Lots of times, when I trapped in Kentucky, I'd spend half the winter without trappin' anythin'. Then, all of a sudden, I was trappin' everythin'. Had to work all the next day just stretchin' the hides."

I wasn't listening. My ears seemed to have closed as I stared at the poor rabbit. I was ashamed of my feelings. Why couldn't I be more like Pa?

"Early season pelts aren't worth much anyway," Pa went on, trying to make me feel better. "Fur gets real thick in colder weather."

I looked up and tried to smile. "Reckon you're right, Pa. Just think of how much money we'd be a-losin' by not waitin' till their pelts are thicker. Best we don't trap for a spell. It ain't worth it."

An odd look appeared on Pa's face. He turned and headed down the trail. I hurried to catch him, but he was twenty feet in front and moving fast. I didn't know what I'd said that made him feel so bad. My breath was white in the air as I raced after him. When I caught up with him I accidentally stepped on his snowshoes and he fell, face down. I laughed and helped Pa regain his footing. Instead of laughing with me, as he normally would, Pa turned and glided silently across the frozen snow.

The remaining traps were empty. I was secretly glad to head home empty-handed. But I still hadn't figured out why there was such hurt in Pa's eyes. Trying to make him at least smile before we reached the house, I said, "Ma didn't want rabbit stew for supper, anyway."

Pa's laughter made me feel better. Ma must have heard us coming because she was standing on the veranda with her coat on. "You've come home empty-handed," she said. "I'm surprised you're both laughing!"

"Has something to do with rabbit stew," Pa said, nudging me. "Come on. Let's get some hot cocoa, son." We kicked off our snowshoes and leaned them against the house so they wouldn't freeze flat on the wooden veranda. Pa handed Ma the rifle and put his arm around my shoulders. The three of us entered the warm house together.

Sitting around the fireplace, Ma listened as our story was retold at least three times. I cleaned the rifle and placed it back in its cradle. When the trap line story finally ended, I asked, "Have you seen Hoppy? I looked for her on the way in."

Ma smiled and touched my arm. "Let's you and I take a carrot out to the shed and check on Hoppy and Joey before it gets dark. Let your old pa rest a bit. Besides, I haven't seen you all day."

"Sure, Ma. Let me get my boots back on."

We walked quietly together to the shed. "Hoppy?" I circled the haystack calling her name and found both kangaroos looking up at me, expecting food.

"Here, give her this carrot. Joey's still drinking milk," said Ma. Hoppy took the carrot with her front paws and started munching.

"I'll see if there's any eggs," I said.

"I checked when I fed the chickens. The nests were empty."

I turned for the house.

"Casey, wait a moment before going inside. I'd like to know what's wrong."

"What do you mean?"

"I know my son. Something happened today. Want to tell me about it?"

"I hurt Pa's feelings," I answered.

"How?"

"I don't know. We were really happy. Working together like we always do. I even tried to talk exactly like him since you weren't around to correct my English. Maybe he thought I was making fun of him."

"Were you?"

"No, of course not."

"Your pa is the wisest man I know; he just never had the opportunity to finish school. He was the oldest and had to support his younger sister and mother when your grandpa ran off to California. Your pa feels bad because he speaks poorly. He's a good man, and loves you very much."

"I love him, too," I answered. "And I won't hurt his feelings ever again."

"Just be yourself, that's all Pa wants you to be. He wants you to be educated."

I nodded. "Thanks, Ma, I understand now." I turned for the house. "I never knew Pa had a younger sister."

"She was born about the time your grandpa arrived in Australia. I've never met her and your pa hasn't seen her for twenty years. I haven't seen my brothers or sisters since we moved to Montana from Ohio. The last letter I got was over a year ago."

"Don't you miss them?"

"Every day," Ma answered. "We were really a close family. But moving away was my doing, so I can't complain. I chose to make a life with your pa, for better or for worse."

"Wish I had a brother or sister," I said.

"God gave us only one child, but at least He gave us the pick of the litter."

Ma's words made me feel good. As we left the shed, I couldn't help but glance at Lady's empty yard.

"Miss her?" Ma asked.

"Especially in the morning when I look out my window, and she ain't–*isn't* there. And at school during recess, and when I ride Lop Ears home at night. I worry about her all the time. I wish we'd gone looking for her rather than going trapping today."

Ma and me went inside and stood in front of the fire with Pa, warming our hands.

"Pa ... I didn't know you had a sister," I said.

Pa glanced at Ma. She shrugged.

"Her name's Elisabeth," Pa said. "We called her Betty. She ran away with a Yankee soldier when she was about sixteen, one of George Custer's men. Custer was in Kentucky to stop the carpetbaggers from stealin' everythin' after the war. When the General and his men was sent to Chicago to maintain order after the great fire, Betty went with them. Custer came back to Kentucky, but Betty never did. Momma died from sharecroppin' the next year so I traveled north through Ohio lookin' for my sister. That's when I met your ma. Never did see Betty again. I don't think my daddy even knew he had a daughter."

The fire snapped, tossing a hot coal at my foot. I kicked it back into the fire. "I wonder how Lady's doing?" My voice sounded hollow inside my head, as if I were talking into an empty gorge. More firmly, I said, "I hope she's all right."

"Probably better than we are," Pa said. "I doubt if there's much snow in the deep gorge where you left her. If this weather holds, we'll have a warmin' by next weekend. Maybe we can travel up that way. Have a look-see."

I nodded. "Let's plan on next Sunday."

"Feel like a game of checkers?" Pa asked.

"I'll get the board," I answered, suddenly feeling better.

"I get to play the winner," Ma said.

"This time, I ain't a-gonna let Casey win," Pa said.

"You don't *let* me win! I beat you flat out!"

He just gave me his Pa smile.

———————

The winter passed slowly by. Every Sunday morning, so long as the weather was fine, I searched for Lady, but I didn't find her – or Moonrunner. I was very worried. Early Saturday morning and late Sunday afternoon, I ran the trap line. I kept trying to force myself to like trapping, but I knew that all the forces in the world could never change my mind. I felt as if I were betraying the family, so I pretended just to make Pa happy.

I was plodding through the newly fallen snow early one Saturday morning, worrying about Lady and Moonrunner instead of having my mind on trapping. The first half of the line had been empty as usual. But as I continued towards the Mitta Mitta River I saw a tan-colored animal in the snow near the next trap. There was red blood everywhere on the white snow. I fell to my knees, suddenly weak. I felt sick.

A dingo or something had eaten a part of the possum. The poor thing didn't have a chance. I leaned the rifle against a nearby tree and opened the jaws of the trap to free the dead possum just as a black shadow flashed across the snow. Teeth ripped at my head and cut my ear. The wild dog's momentum knocked me over. It growled fiercely and attacked again. I lunged for the rifle. Falling short, I dropped into the snow just as the animal attacked. I kicked the dog in the stomach. My vision blurred. Leaping to my feet, I yanked off my gloves and felt blood on my face. The dog stood in front of me, snarling. It suddenly lunged again. Stumbling backwards across the snow with the dog biting my coat, I grabbed the rifle and swung it like a baseball bat. The dog yelped once and fell in the snow, but quickly sprung up again. Blood blinded me.

I swung the rifle again, missing wildly. The dog lunged, hitting me hard on the chest and knocking me over. Teeth locked onto the back of my thick collar, right at my throat, pulling me to the ground. I rolled out of my sheepskin coat and for a moment the dog fought my coat. I hit it as hard as I could on the back of the neck.

The dog charged again. I spun the rifle around and fired without aiming. Stunned, I fell against the tree and wiped the blood from my eyes. As the dog hobbled towards me with its teeth snapping together, I landed a fierce blow across its nose. The dog collapsed into the snow.

The battle was suddenly over. I fell beside the dog, dizzy, too weak to stand. My blood mixed with the possum's blood and the dog's blood. Billows of vapor escaped my mouth as I gulped cold air. My lungs burned. The dog and I stared at each other. It was growling, but not moving.

Dragging myself across the snow on my stomach, I freed the dead possum from the trap. "I'm sorry, I'm sorry," I said, over and over.

I buried the possum's remains in the snow beside the tree. Afterwards, I put on my ripped coat and blinked stupidly at the dog. It stared at me without blinking, growling menacingly, wanting its dinner back.

Packing snow against my cut head and ear, I picked up the rifle and stumbled for home.

I called for help, but my voice became weaker and weaker. In my mind, I saw Pa playing checkers with Ma in front of the warm fire. The blood wouldn't stop flowing. I collapsed into the snow and wiped the blood from my eyes. I was nearly home. The house was just up the hill in a clump of trees. I yelled, but no sound came out. I yelled again. My voice merely squeaked in my throat like a puppy dog's whimper. I tried crawling across the snow. My strength was gone. Wiggling the rifle from my shoulder, I fired a three-shot distress signal before falling back into the snow.

Pa came running down the hill and rolled me over. "Casey! What happened?"

"Wild dog," I whispered. "Can't stop the blood."

Pa quickly removed his scarf and placed it over my head wounds. "Press this tight!"

"Hands frozen … can't," I answered.

"You've got to! I'm going back for the sledge. We must get you to the doctor in Omeo."

Pa galloped Girlie through the snow. Ma sat in the back of the sledge holding my head in her lap. She was pressing rags against my wounds. The trip seemed especially long.

When the doctor had finished patching me back together, I heard him tell Ma, "He's lost a great deal of blood. Thank God it was cold. Keep him in bed. I want to see him in three days to check the stitches."

While I was healing, I had more time to think about the trap line. Killing the possum was enough trapping to last me a lifetime. Trapping animals was like putting my own spirit in a locked box and hiding it in a dark corner. I vowed to never again trap another animal.

The first Saturday after the stitches were removed, without telling Pa, I sprung every trap and left them closed. On Wednesday, Pa would patiently reset the traps. Then, on Thursday and Friday at school, I prayed no animals would be trapped. On Saturday I would spring them again.

The snow melted as the weather warmed, only to cover the ground again just before spring. I had kept my secret all winter. One Saturday morning I stepped onto the veranda to put on my snowshoes. Pa followed me. "Such a nice day. I think I'll go along," he said.

I didn't look up from tying on my snowshoes. "That's all right, Pa. I can do it by myself."

"Won't take me two shakes," Pa said. He grabbed his coat and closed the front door. "I'll carry the rifle." He strapped on his snowshoes and stepped off the veranda. "I had a difficult time resetting the traps last Wednesday. Really snowing! Every one of them was sprung, just like before. I can't understand it."

"Maybe some smart wombat has learned how to spring the traps," I said.

"Sure wish we could teach him to set them again," Pa answered, laughing.

I looked to the shed, as I always did, to say goodbye to Hoppy, but I couldn't see her. I yelled, "Get out of bed, Hoppy! The day's half over!"

Pa broke a trail through the snow until we reached the bridge, where I took the lead. As we approached the first trap, I saw a large animal curled up on the snow. I froze. The animal wasn't moving.

Pa stepped around me, grinning widely. "You've done it, Case. You've trapped a big somethin' this time."

"You set the traps, Pa, it wasn't me."

"Kind of a mutual effort, wouldn't you say? Real teamwork." Pa rushed forwards and abruptly stopped. I heard him suck in his breath. "Oh, my God!"

"What's wrong?" I asked.

"It's Hoppy."

Stumbling in my snowshoes, I tripped and crawled across the snow. "No! No! It can't be!"

Pa dropped onto his knees beside the kangaroo. "She's alive, but she's cold. The trap's really cut her leg open." He stood, handed me the Winchester and pointed at Hoppy.

"I'm not going to shoot her, Pa!"

"I'm not askin' you to shoot her! Stick the barrel carefully

144

in the trap and twist it open while I lift her out. We must get her to the house. That wound's got to be doctored."

"How's Joey?" I asked.

"Can't tell. Twist open the trap and let's have a look-see."

I stuck the rifle barrel between the jaws of the trap and twisted. Pa pulled the kangaroo free and rolled her over. When the little joey poked his head from Hoppy's pouch, I shouted with relief. "Joey's alive! I didn't kill Joey!"

"Run back to the shed. Bring that piece of canvas coverin' the sledge. Hoppy's too heavy for us to carry. We'll drag her up the hill."

———◦◦◦———

That evening, Hoppy rested in the sitting room in front of the fireplace. Her eyes were closed, but I could tell that she wasn't sleeping. Little Joey had hidden in my bedroom and wouldn't come out. After having rabbit stew for dinner, I sat on the floor beside Hoppy, stroking her side. Pa looked up from his woodcarving and said, "That's about all we can do for now, son. I think she's goin' be fine. Time for bed."

"She's too hot," I said. "She's not used to being inside."

"Can't put her back in the shed," he answered. "Too cold. She'd freeze."

"I'll get some hay," Ma said. "Let's make a bed for her in the corner." She put on her coat and left the room.

"It's been a long day, son. Get to bed, and send Joey out to be with his mama."

Ma returned with her arms full of hay and dropped it in the corner of the sitting room. Pa and I dragged Hoppy across the room and carefully lifted her onto the hay. I kept stroking Hoppy's neck, trying to delay going to bed for as long as possible.

"Are you going to look for Lady in the morning?" Ma asked.

I shrugged. "I might give Lop Ears a rest." How could I search for Lady with Hoppy hurting so badly? Besides, I had something else to do in the morning.

"Then I won't fix your lunch," Ma said.

"I'll keep my eye on her, son. Get to bed."

I entered my room and found Joey sleeping in the middle of my bed. Startled, he scurried into the sitting room.

Ma stuck her head into the room. "Goodnight, son. Hoppy's going to be fine, so get some sleep. I'll see you in the morning." She closed the door. I was left in the darkness, staring up at the ceiling.

Eventually, when the house became very quiet, I eased from my room. Pa had banked the fire for the night to keep it burning low.

Hoppy watched me cross the dark room. I think she was glad to see me. I curled up beside her and petted her tenderly. I whispered, "How you feeling, Hoppy? I'm sorry you got caught in my trap. But it wasn't my fault. I want you to know that it wasn't my fault. I sprung all the traps, every Saturday morning. Pa set the trap that caught you, it wasn't me."

A chair suddenly scraped the floor, scaring me. My heart raced. In the shadows, Pa's figure slowly stood and walked towards me. "Is that right, Casey? You kicked the traps closed?"

I looked at his angry face scowling at me in the firelight. For a brief moment, I saw a part of Pa I didn't understand. His hard stare frightened me so badly that I couldn't speak. I knew I was in for a big whipping.

"Why?" When I didn't answer, Pa said, "Casey! Speak! Why did you do it?"

"'Cause I hate trapping," I screamed. "I can feel their pain inside my heart!"

Pa was fuming. He kept quiet and sat down beside me. "I wasted a lot of time settin' those traps. Last week I went out in a snowstorm! I thought we were workin' together. Do you think that's fair?"

"No, sir." I added, "Pa? I'd hoped you would understand."

Pa shook his head. "I'll never understand. Your grandpa earned enough money trappin' to send for us. And I sold furs to support my family in Kentucky. You could've saved us both a lot of trouble by tellin' me sooner."

I felt cornered. "I tried to tell ya, but ya wouldn't listen. I ain't like you or Grandpa. I hate trappin'!"

Ma entered the room, putting on her robe. "What's all this ruckus?" she asked.

"Casey's been kickin' the traps closed all winter after I set 'em. No wonder he didn't trap anythin'!"

Ma sat on the floor beside Pa and leaned against him. "Is that right, son?"

I nodded. "Yes," I mumbled.

Pa glanced at Ma. No one spoke for a long time.

Finally Ma said, "It was wrong of you to let your pa go out every week resetting the traps. And last week in a snowstorm! Do you know it was wrong?"

I nodded. "I'm sorry, Ma." Tears of shame dripped from my eyes. I sniffled. "After the possum died in my trap, something changed in me. The first thing I did when I got well was to kick the traps shut."

"And on Sunday afternoon after searching for Lady, you pretended to run the trap line, when all the time the traps were closed?"

I nodded.

"I'm really disappointed in you. You should've told us." When I didn't answer, she said, "Casey. I know it's important for you to stand up for what you believe, but not by lying to your family. You could've been doing your homework, or helping me in the kitchen, or helping Pa instead of wasting time trapping. Surviving on a homestead is hard work! We all have to do our share."

Again I didn't answer.

Ma said, "Apologize to your pa, right now!"

Still looking at the floor, I mumbled, "I'm sorry, Pa."

"That's not good enough. Look at him." Ma said sternly.

I looked up. The hardness was gone from Pa's face. His

eyes silently reached out to me, pulling me back into his heart.

He asked, "What are you goin' to do about the money for the race next year, and feeding Lady?"

"I need a pound to enter the race, that's all. And we'll have enough hay from the bottomland along the creek for all the animals next winter."

"You got it all figured out, huh, like you've been thinkin' about it for a spell."

"I have," I answered.

"How will you earn the money?" Ma asked.

"I'll get a job in town ... or brumby-run with Ernie ..."

"We've got too many spring chores for you to go gallivantin' across the high plains after brumbies," Pa said.

I petted Hoppy again without looking at Pa. I couldn't stand the guilt I was feeling for disappointing the family. "Think Lady's all right?"

"Casey, don't change the subject. It takes teamwork as a family to survive. If you're goin' to spring the traps after I set 'em, there's no sense settin' 'em."

I nodded solemnly. "In the morning, I'm going to bring in all the traps."

"I'll go with you," Pa said.

"I can do it alone."

"So can I. But together we can do it much faster. With you springin' the traps and me disconnectin' 'em from the tree."

It was quiet for a long time. Little Joey stretched a hind leg and yawned. Pa said, "Son, I've been thinkin' ... I'm not

goin' to trap any more. And you're not goin' to trap anymore
… and you worked hard gettin' the traps back in shape."

"What are you getting at, Pa?" I asked.

"Those are darn good traps. Should be worth somethin'."

"You mean, sell Grandpa's traps?"

Pa shrugged. "Will you ever trap again?"

"No, never," I said.

"And I know my daddy won't. Let's go into Omeo and see
what kind of price they'll bring."

"I don't want anyone to use those traps on animals."

"Good steel is hard to get," Pa said. "I reckon the
blacksmith can turn them into somethin' more useful."

The dozen traps with their long chains attached sold for
three pounds at the Omeo blacksmith. When Pa received
the money, he handed it me. "This money's yours, son. You
worked hard for it."

I held the coins in my hand. "I'll keep a pound for the
race. Another pound should buy some oats and hay for Lady
after we catch her."

"What'll you do with the rest of the money?"

"I want to get some tobacco for your pipe and some
pretty material for Ma to make a new dress. Can you help me
select the material, Pa? I'm not too good at that sort of thing."

"I'm not either, son. That's somethin' about us menfolk.
But between us, I imagine we'll do just fine." Pa put his arm
on my shoulder and we walked the rest of the way into Omeo.

★ CHAPTER THIRTEEN ★

First Spring

As spring approached and new grasses changed the colors of the hills on the way to school from drab brown to green, I became anxious about capturing Lady. Brumby-running with Ernie last Easter had given me confidence, but I wasn't sure I could build a trap strong enough to hold Moonrunner while I cut Lady from his other mares.

My woodcutting chores around the homestead slowed as the weather warmed, and the ground for our early crops was still too wet to plow, so I had more time to venture away from the homestead on weekends. Several times, I rode Old Lop Ears into the hidden gorge looking for Lady, but it was impossible to separate Lady's tracks from the brumbies' tracks. It looked like she had lost her shoes.

When the snow finally melted, Pa and I hitched Girlie to the bullock wagon early one morning and loaded it with two axes, ropes, shovels, a huge hammer to drive stakes in the ground, and a large canvas for the trapdoor. We headed down Bingo Munjie Creek towards the Mitta Mitta River. The road along the creek was still muddy in places. Several times we got out to help Girlie pull the heavy wagon along. We finally reached the swollen river about noon.

"What do you think, Pa?" I asked. We remained in the wagon, watching old trees and weeds floating by in the murky floodwater.

"Looks kinda dangerous," he answered.

"I rode across on Lop Ears last Sunday," I said. "The ford is straight in front of Girlie. Just keep her aimed towards that dead tree on the far side. That's what I do."

"Was the river this muddy when you crossed last weekend?" Pa asked.

"Seems like it's running a little faster now, and there's more drift wood floating by." I stepped down from the wagon. "I'm going to wade across to see what it's like."

"That ain't a good idea, son."

"Don't worry, Pa, I can swim."

"I know you can swim 'cause I learned you. What if a log hits you or somethin'?"

"It ain't going to do us any good to be stuck on this side of the river and have the work on that side. We have to get the wagon across!"

"I agree, so don't get so danged cantankerous! I'm sure glad your ma ain't here to see this. Take off your breeches. No sense getting 'em wet. If you get knocked down, don't fight the current. Just float along and slowly paddle to land. I'll pick you up downstream."

"Okay, Pa." I stripped, held my breeches on top of my head, and stepped into the cold water. The current wasn't bad near the bank, but it became stronger as I waded into the middle where the water was just above my knees. Several times I pushed a dead tree away with one hand while balancing on the slippery rocks beneath. But I easily made it to the opposite side. Turning, I shouted. "It's okay, Pa. Not too strong."

Pa snapped the reins and Girlie started into the water. Halfway across, a branch floated against her belly. She started jumping in her traces and squealing as though the tree were a snake.

"Easy girl!" Pa said. "Casey, get the branch away from her belly!"

I dropped my breeches and rushed into the swollen river. Girlie was near panic by the time I reached her. I carefully worked the branch away from her stomach and let it float downstream. She was still nervous. I held her leads firmly with both hands. My soothing words finally quieted her.

"Get on her back and ride her across," Pa said.

I jumped up so I was balanced on my stomach over Girlie's withers and spun my leg around to sit up. "Come on, Girlie, just a little bit further. See the riverbank? I'll give you some oats."

Girlie took an unsure step, then another. Eventually, she pulled the wagon out of the river. Meanwhile, I was freezing. As soon as I had put on my breeches, I pulled out a handful of the oats that I'd brought for Lady and fed it to Girlie.

By nightfall we had chosen an area beyond the spring in the hidden gorge and built the funnel and part of the trapdoor.

"Good day's work, huh, Pa?" I collapsed near the spring. "We did about as much as ten of Ernie's station hands."

"Sure was. I'm bushed," Pa answered. "Tomorrow we'll finish the yard and hang the trapdoor."

"Don't forget the two trails out of this gorge," I said. "One's over there, just beyond that big boulder. The other is up over the spur, that way."

"You're right. Wouldn't do much good to trap Moonrunner then watch him dance across the spur into the sunset. He'd never come back this way again."

"What happens if we don't catch him by tomorrow night?" I asked.

"I told your ma we might be an extra couple days. I brought along the rifle for food. We'll make it, don't worry."

I was bone tired, too tired to eat anything. I wearily washed my face in the spring and stumbled towards the wagon. Pulling out my bedroll, I looked for a place to settle for the night.

"Just a minute, Casey," Pa said. He untied an extra canvas and rolled it beneath the wagon. I shook out my blankets on top of the canvas, crawled under the wagon, and tried my best to stay awake long enough to make plans for tomorrow. But the long hard day had been too much for me. The last thing I remember was listening to the rhythm of Pa's snoring.

At daybreak, after eating a cold breakfast to keep the smell of cooking food out of the gorge, we went directly to work. My arms and back were sore from cutting brush and trimming the skinny trees to make the post and rail yard. I could've used one of Ma's hot baths. Pa groaned all through breakfast without complaining, so I know he must've been sore, too.

By mid-morning the trapdoor was rigged and tested. The yard took no time at all to put up because the trees had been cut and trimmed the previous day. We worked without stopping to block off the two escape routes. By late afternoon, the trap was ready.

"You want to drop the trapdoor or go find Moonrunner?" Pa asked.

"It'll be dark in a couple of hours," I answered. "Let's wait till tomorrow."

"You called him Moonrunner 'cause he runs at night. Now's the best time to find him. If you're too tired, I'll go."

I was exhausted and anxious, but I answered, "I'll go. I know the hidden trails over the spurs."

"Think you're right," Pa said.

Remembering how uncomfortable I had been hiding beside the trapdoor waiting for Ernie to drive in the brumbies, I said, "I'll be gone a while, so don't fall asleep."

Pa grinned. "Don't worry, son, I'll be ready."

"Think they can smell you hiding in the trap?"

"Heat from the open spur draws the cooler air up the gorge. I'll be downwind. The first they'll know I'm here will be when I lower the trapdoor."

I laughed. I saddled Girlie and painfully mounted. "See you later, Pa."

Riding out the mouth of the gorge, I circled downriver to another gorge that led up to the spur. Once on top, I reversed my direction and looked down on our trap from the ridge just above. No brumbies yet. No sign of Pa, either. The trap looked natural, as if bushes were growing on the gorge floor instead of funnel walls and a post and rail yard.

I rode long after dark. There were sounds of brumbies breaking brush in front of me and I found fresh tracks everywhere, but I didn't see any horses. It was frustrating. Where was Moonrunner? Where was Lady? Two miles downriver from the hidden gorge, I decided to call it quits for the night. My back was stiff from the cold. My legs ached from sitting in the saddle so long.

I walked Girlie slowly along the river. Her head was hanging to the ground; mine was hanging on my chest. Girlie was tired from pulling the wagon and climbing in and out of these rugged gorges. I was tired from cutting wood, riding in the cold and worrying about Lady all winter. Most of all I was tired from disappointment. I had thought catching Lady would be easy.

Just before entering the hidden gorge, I dismounted and let Girlie drink while I sat on a fallen tree and watched the last glimmer of light disappear behind Mt. Hotham.

The narrow gorge was dark and forbidding as Girlie picked her way along the trail towards the campsite. When we arrived, I was upset to see Pa had a small fire going. He was cooking supper. If I could smell the hot food cooking, so could Moonrunner!

Pa looked up and smiled at me as I dismounted. I removed Girlie's saddle and hung it on the sideboard of the wagon.

"Hello, son. Where'd you go?" Pa spoke casually, as if we were on a regular camping trip. I still couldn't believe he was actually cooking dinner.

"Why the fire? Moonrunner can smell a fire ten miles away!"

"Have you looked in the trap?" Pa grinned.

My heart leaped into my throat. The trapdoor was closed! I'd been too tired to look as I rode up the gorge. Suddenly, I felt no pain at all. I ran to the brush enclosure to find it was full of wild horses.

"You caught them! You caught them!"

"It was you. They came in just after dark, runnin' like somethin' was chasin 'em. Moonrunner must've kept just out of sight from you all afternoon. Moonrunner chose his favorite canyon, thinkin' he could escape out the back way. Your trap really got him. Ernie sure taught you well."

"Was Lady with them?" I asked.

"Couldn't tell. It was too dark. We'll have to wait till mornin'. They ain't goin' anywhere. We got 'em."

———•◦•———

It was several hours before Moonrunner stopped charging the trap to test its strength and settled down for the night. It took about as long for me to relax. I pretended to sleep. In the fire's glow, I could see that Pa was worried. He was on his back, being very quiet. I could almost hear his eyes blinking. Maybe he hadn't seen Lady in the mob and didn't want to tell me. Maybe he's thinking, "What will I say if Lady's not there? But she's just got to be there. She's got to."

At dawn, I rolled from beneath the wagon without waking Pa and quietly climbed a large boulder near the trapdoor. I had slept in my boots. Pa finally spotted me looking down into the yard.

"Casey, what do you see down there?"

"The most pretty sight in the whole world," I answered. "Lady's in the yard. We got her back."

Pa laughed with relief. "Well don't just stand there. Throw a rope around her and let's go home."

I slid down to join Pa. He had a rope in his hand. He said, "I'll go into the corral. Moonrunner looks like he could be awfully mean."

"Moonrunner doesn't know you, Pa. I think he'll remember me. Let me try first."

Pa said, "Sounds logical." He handed me the coiled rope. "Stay near the trapdoor. If Moonrunner charges, dive for the canvas and I'll pull you under."

I pictured Moonrunner trampling my legs as Pa tried to pull me clear. But I knew that I had a better chance than Pa, so I got some sugar to entice Lady and returned to the yard. I tucked the coiled lead rope carefully into the back of my breeches to hide it from Lady's eyes and eased through the canvas door into the yard. I stood quietly just inside, trying not to show the fear that I felt. Moonrunner didn't move as I talked softly, holding out the sugar.

"Remember me, Moonrunner? Easy now, easy does it. I'm not going to hurt you." The stallion stepped in front of his mares. "I just want Lady back. You can keep your mares. But Lady's mine. I'm thanking you for taking care of her."

Moonrunner's legs quivered. Suddenly, he lunged at me with his ears lowered and his hooves flying. I stood my ground, unmoving. Moonrunner abruptly stopped less than ten feet away. His nostrils flared; his eyes were wild. I glanced over my shoulder, but didn't see Pa.

"You there, Pa?"

"Hiding behind the canvas," he whispered. "I don't want Moonrunner to see me."

Relieved, I turned to face the black stallion again. My throat tightened. I forced myself to remain calm. Pa says animals can smell fear. Sweat rolled down my face and stung my eyes. My arm ached from holding the sugar in front of me. Moonrunner whirled and ran back to protect his mares. Without warning, the wild stallion charged again. I dived for the canvas, but tripped. I slammed into the canvas and rolled awkwardly backwards.

Dirt flew as Moonrunner planted his hooves beside my head. I looked up into flaring nostrils. His hot breath blasted my face. I was at the black stallion's mercy. Moonrunner looked down at me, staring right into my eyes.

"What's happening?" Pa asked.

"Moonrunner remembers me," I whispered. "I'm all right." I started talking to Moonrunner again and slowly stood.

Moonrunner backed towards his mares and moved to the far side of the corral. He nickered once. At that moment I felt like my senses had been heightened. I knew exactly what Moonrunner was doing. He was permitting me to coax Lady out, but wasn't going to offer help. If I failed, he'd refuse to let her go.

I stepped away from the gate and circled to my right, holding the sugar and talking to Lady as I moved. She was behind the mares, next to a vertical wall. "Lady, Lady. It's me, Casey. Come get your sugar. Sugar, Lady. I've got sugar here."

I talked as if my whole life depended on that moment. I wasn't aware of where I was or whether Pa was still behind me or whether it was night or day.

"You haven't forgotten me, have you, girl?" I whistled softly, my special whistle just for her, and kept my eye on Moonrunner in case he changed his mind and suddenly charged. But Moonrunner stood very still, watching.

As I neared the mares, they moved away to stand behind the black stallion. One mare remained standing alone. It was Lady. What a beautiful sight! But she didn't come closer.

While she hesitated, I slowly approached with the sugar. She took one step forwards, then another. Lady's nose twitched as she smelled the sugar. Catching herself, she stopped and nickered at Moonrunner. The stallion remained quiet. Unsure of what to do, Lady looked back at me, then at Moonrunner again. I waited until she was looking at me before I walked slowly towards her. This time, she nickered at me and trotted over to eat the sugar. I quickly slipped the rope around her neck and tied it to a tree limb.

"Okay, Pa. I got her. Open the trap and release the brumbies."

"Are you sure?"

"I'm sure. I made a promise to Moonrunner. Let him go."

Pa untied the canvas. When it fell to the ground, Moonrunner didn't move. Pa dragged the canvas out of the doorway and cautiously entered the yard. The stallion reared on his hind legs and whinnied. When his forelegs hit the ground, Moonrunner spun sharply and circled behind his mares, biting several on the flank to force them through the open doorway. He was the last to leave. Once outside the gate, he stopped to look back.

I held Lady as I looked at the stallion. A bond had been formed between us. I could feel it and I'm sure the stallion felt it, too. "Goodbye, Moonrunner. Thanks for taking care of Lady for me. I'll stop by to see you this summer. If you ever need anything, let me know." Moonrunner whinnied loudly as he galloped down the gorge after his mares.

I untied Lady and led her out of the yard. "We got Lady back. She sure looks ragged, but we got her back."

"She looks pretty good, son. That's just her long winter coat. A lot of currying, some warmer weather and a few oats, she'll be a different horse in two weeks."

I led her out of the trap. Lady kept looking down the gorge after Moonrunner. Pa said, "You'd better not ride her. She could be a little wild."

Tying her to the back of the wagon, I answered, "I'll spend some time with her this afternoon so she can get to know me again before school tomorrow."

We broke up the trap and the two barricades that blocked the escape routes out of the canyon and headed for home. Once we'd crossed the river, I sat backwards on the tailgate so I could watch Lady trotting behind.

I had Lady back and she was healthy. I had the money to enter the Omeo race next year. And I was beginning to make friends. It was going to be a great summer, even if I couldn't get used to the idea of a hot Christmas!

★ CHAPTER FOURTEEN ★

Captured

Summer had passed, it had been one of the best ever. I'd spent every moment I could with Lady. But the big surprise was that I had spent nearly as much time with Frank. He was now my best friend. We'd discovered a limestone cave near the Mitta Mitta River where we'd played pirates all day, and I told him stories about my family crossing the Pacific Ocean by boat. For my birthday, we'd ridden to Omeo just to go roller skating.

Now school was back and the two mile race was just two weeks away. Lady wasn't running well. I was really worried. I galloped her up the hill to school every day, but she was lazy. She needed a bigger challenge, a challenge that would really make her work hard. So I wrote another note at school and passed it around.

I need help training Lady for the Omeo race. If you are interested, meet me in the yard after school.

Thanks,
Casey

When I got the note back, Mike had written in bold letters across the bottom, "We're all betting your nag will finish last, just like last year. Ha! Ha!" Below Mike's note, little Gracie had written, "Mike is so stupid!" Somehow, the note from Gracie made me not care about Mike.

Frank, Maggie, and Mary were waiting at the yard. I knew that Frank would be there. And it really made me feel good that Maggie and Mary were willing to help. Mike and Jimmy were across the pen saddling their horses.

Maggie said, "You serious about entering Lady in the race?"

I nodded. "Yep, but Lady doesn't like to run unless she's racing other horses."

Mike laughed. "Bloody bag of bones will never finish the race. I'll see to that!"

"Shut up, Mike!" Mary yelled. She glared at Mike for a moment, then turned to me. "We'll help you, Casey. Just tell us what to do."

"Every day after school we'll race down the road to the Anderson Place."

"Lady's too fast," Frank said. "It won't be much of a race."

"I'll give you a head start. That way, Lady will work harder."

Jimmy led his saddled horse through the open gate. Mike suddenly yelled and flapped his arms wildly. Our horses bolted through the open gate and scattered.

Mike strutted to his horse, sneering. "You won't be racing today, Casey Jenner! It'll be dark before you find Lady. Hope you walk home." Laughing loudly, he and Jimmy rode away.

———•◦•———

Early Saturday morning, about a week before the Omeo Rodeo, Lady whinnied loudly as I approached the yard. She was telling me that it was time to visit Moonrunner. And I agreed with her. Ma and Pa were making another trip to Omeo, but didn't need me to go along. I saddled her in the shed and spent a little time with the kangaroos. Hoppy's leg had healed. Joey still didn't like to be petted. The baby kangaroo had grown and was unable to climb back into its mother's pouch.

I stuffed my lunch into a saddlebag, mounted and trotted Lady down the dirt rode towards Bingo Munjie Creek. As soon as I was out of sight of the house, I slowed Lady to a gentle walk and put my right leg over the saddle. "No sense rushing, girl. We've got all day."

It was one of those perfect days for riding. I thought about riding up hill to my hideout, but decided against it. "Can't do that, girl," I said. "Moonrunner's waiting to see us." A gentle breeze carried the smell of wild flowers. I filled my lungs with fresh air and gazed at the puffy white clouds drifting aimlessly across the sky.

"Look, Lady, that cloud looks like a rabbit eating a carrot." As the wind altered the formation of the clouds, the rabbit changed into an Apache Indian with two feathers sticking in his hair. I daydreamed lazily all the way to the Mitta Mitta and waded Lady across. Without being reined, she turned up the trail that she knew so well. There were no fresh tracks around the old trap. "Don't worry, girl, he's here somewhere." Lady continued up the steep trail on the far end of the gorge and walked along the spur to the next gorge.

When I looked down from the top of the spur, my lazy, carefree day suddenly changed.

"Someone's built a brumby trap down there, Lady!"

I wheeled Lady around, retraced our tracks to the Mitta Mitta and entered the next gorge. I dismounted to examine the new trap. "It looks like Ernie's work. I'll bet he's captured Moonrunner. We'd better pay Mr. Parkes a visit, right now!"

I leaped into the saddle. As soon as we crossed the river, I put Lady into a fast run and galloped past my house without slowing down.

There didn't seem to be any activity around Mr. Parkes' station as I rode in. I headed to the shed and tied Lady to a snubbing ring near the door. I could hear yelling and shouting coming from the stockyard, so I ran to the five-railed brumby-busting ring and forced my way to the top rail.

Moonrunner had a halter on and was snubbed tightly against the center post with a blindfold over his eyes. A man with a large, floppy hat nervously tried to climb in the saddle. Moonrunner circled away. I spotted Ernie sitting on the top rail on the opposite side of the yard. I scrambled down and ran to join him.

"G'day, Casey. Long time, no see. What brings you over this way?"

"Thought I'd see if you had any brumbies. Having trouble with the black stallion?"

"Sure am. Like nothing we've ever caught before. The bloke trying to get in the saddle is a buckjumper from Ovens Valley. If he can't ride him, I don't know what we'll do."

"Turn him loose," I said.

"Can't do that. Mr. Parkes would have my neck. He wants him busted, one way or another."

"Where'd you catch him?" I asked.

"North of your place, across the Mitta Mitta. About a week ago."

"Did you see another trap in the next gorge?"

"Sure did. I didn't use it though. I didn't want to take advantage of someone else's work."

"It would have been all right," I said.

Ernie turned to face me. "What do you mean?" he asked.

"I made that trap to recapture Lady." As Ernie listened, I told him about Lady wintering with Moonrunner and how I had caught and released him to be with his mares.

"I'm sorry, Casey, I feel terrible. If I'd known, I'd have turned him loose, too. Now, Mr. Parkes wants him broken. When we couldn't do it after trying all week, he sent for that jumper down there. He's not having much luck, either."

In the yard, the buckjumper had just climbed in the saddle and was waiting for the station hand holding the lead rope to pull the blindfold. "Let 'er go!" the buckjumper yelled.

Moonrunner spun around and jumped high in the air. He twisted his hind legs in one direction, his forelegs in another, and bent his head down between his legs to arch his back. When Moonrunner hit the ground he was going a different direction, springing sideways like a mountain lion jumping at a deer. The buckjumper flew through the air and landed face down in the dirt ten feet away. The station hands laughed as the jumper dusted himself with his beaten-up hat. He limped over to where I was sitting with Ernie.

"That no-good brumby! I'll teach him! Get two draft horses and strap the stallion between them. I'm going to wear him out before I try that again."

Soon, two of the heaviest old plugs were hitched together with Moonrunner snubbed firmly between. The stallion quivered in anticipation of more rough treatment.

When the blindfold was removed, Moonrunner started kicking and bucking, bellowing so loudly they must have heard him in Omeo. The draft horses moved away from the angry black devil between them. When they pulled apart, Moonrunner had room to twist and kick even higher. One of the leather straps gave way under the strain. The stallion jumped high and twisted, landing across the back of one of the draft horses. Moonrunner was suspended with his hind legs barely touching the ground and his forelegs awkwardly kicking in mid-air. His neck was bent sharply backwards with his head still strapped in leather.

"You're gonna kill him!" I yelled. I jumped into the yard. I had to save Moonrunner.

The buckjumper screamed, "Shut up, kid, and get out of here! This ain't none of your business!"

I shoved the buckjumper out of my way and jumped on the back of one of the draft horses, frantically trying to untie the leather from around Moonrunner's neck. It was impossible. The knots were pulled tight with the weight of the black stallion.

"Ernie! I need your knife," I yelled.

Mr. Parkes was suddenly there, watching. He yelled, "Ernie, get out of there! I gave orders to stay clear and let the buckjumper handle everything!"

Ernie didn't listen. He jumped on the other draft horse behind me and handed me the knife. I leaned down between the draft horses to cut the straps. They suddenly moved together, pinning me between them. Ernie dug his heel into the side of one horse and forced them apart so I could finish cutting the leads.

"Stand clear, Ernie. This is the last one!" I yelled. As I cut the final lead, Moonrunner twisted over and fell to the ground. Ernie led the two draft horses out of the yard while I knelt beside Moonrunner. I finished cutting away the leather straps and removed the busting saddle. The black stallion remained on his side, gasping for air.

"Easy, Moonrunner. It's okay. It's okay."

Mr. Parkes was yelling at Ernie. The foreman waited until his boss stopped to breathe and said, "You almost lost your stallion, Mr. Parkes. Good thing Casey had enough sense to free him. I was only helping."

Mr. Parkes was still angry. "Where's that no-good jumper?"

Ernie pointed to the shed. "He went in there a few minutes ago."

Climbing the fence beside Ernie, I watched the buckjumper stride out carrying a heavy metal chain, about three feet long. Mr. Parkes stormed towards the shed. "What are you planning to do with that?"

"I'm gonna show that brumby who's boss!" the buckjumper said.

"Get off my station!" Mr. Parkes said.

"Huh?"

"I said you're finished here. You weren't none too successful, so you're not needed around here anymore." Mr. Parkes turned towards the yard. The buckjumper remained standing sullenly alone in front of the shed with the chain hanging limply in the dirt at his feet. "Ernie, get the man his money. We've got work to do."

Ernie paid the jumper and returned to the yard. I

remained on the fence, thankful to see that Moonrunner was back on his feet. Mr. Parkes had the black stallion snubbed to the center post in the middle of the ring.

"What are you going to do?" Ernie asked.

"None of you could break the stallion, so I'll do it my way. I'm going to break his spirit. Then he'll come around," said Mr. Parkes.

I watched Ernie's face grow angry and his jaw tighten. When Mr. Parkes went into the shed, I asked, "What's it mean, Ernie?"

Ernie spoke without looking at me. "Mr. Parkes is going to beat Moonrunner with a club until he no longer has strength to resist."

"He won't be the same horse! You know that! Please, Ernie, you know Moonrunner's too proud to be broken. He'll die first."

Mr. Parkes heard me begging with Ernie as he returned with a piece of wood in his hand. His temper had cooled down, but I was still frightened. He said, "If you don't want to see the stallion get busted, you'd best go home, boy."

I walked towards Lady feeling frustrated and helpless, a traitor, too weak to stand by a friend. Instead of mounting and riding away in shame, I led Lady back to the yard. Mr. Parkes was going to hear what I had to say.

"You've got to free him, Mr. Parkes. Moonrunner and I have an agreement."

"I can't do that. If I gave all my animals away I'd have no

station at all."

"He's only one horse," I argued. "You have thousands."

"A horse is a horse. I can sell him for something."

I took a deep breath and tightened my jaw. "Mr. Parkes, you know I'm entering Lady in the race next week."

"What does that have to do with the black stallion?" he asked.

I said, "I want to make a bet with you."

"What kind of bet?" Mr. Parkes asked.

"If I win the race, the black stallion is mine. If I lose, you get Lady back." I nearly choked on the words.

"You really play for keeps, don't you, boy?"

Ernie said, "Not much difference in the spirit of the stallion and the spirit of Casey, if you ask me."

Mr. Parkes walked around Lady, letting his hand drag along her side. Lady fidgeted nervously under his touch. "Ernie, come here a minute. Feel her stomach, see if you think what I think."

After a few minutes, Ernie said, "Yep, she's in foal." He quickly told Mr. Parkes how I had wintered Lady with Moonrunner. "That means the black stallion is the father. What a foal that's going to be!"

Mr. Parkes turned to me and said, "Still want to make that bet?"

"Yes, sir. Once said, a bet should stand."

"It's a deal." He shook my hand and turned for the house.

I yelled after him. "Mr. Parkes! You have to leave the black stallion alone until after the race." Mr. Parkes nodded and continued to the house.

"Be careful, Casey," Ernie said. "Mr. Parkes brought three horses in from Melbourne. He's been running them against each other and the clock. They're really fast. A horse, one way or another, doesn't mean much to him. It's the pride, whether it's winning the race or breaking the stallion's spirit. You stand to lose Lady and her foal, and Lady's all you've got. I know I told you Lady was the fastest thing around these parts, but that was last year."

"Will a foal slow her down?"

"A mate of mine was at the Melbourne Cup years ago. It's a two mile race, too. He said that a pregnant mare came in third. It won't slow her down at all."

"Then we'll win, Ernie." I swung into the saddle. "We've just got to. If I don't, Moonrunner will be dead and I won't feel like owning Lady anyway." I spun Lady around and rode away.

★ CHAPTER FIFTEEN ★

The Omeo Race

Last year I had been excited about going to the Omeo Rodeo. But I carried a different feeling with me this year. I sat backwards in the bullock wagon on the way to town, trailing Lady behind on a loose rope. I had chosen not to ride her so she would be fresh and full of energy.

"Do you think she's going to have a foal, Pa, like Ernie says?" I asked.

Pa spoke without turning around. "Could be, son. Ernie really knows horses."

"Ernie said it won't slow her down," I said, "but I'm still worried."

"How did she feel when you ran her last week?"

I moved forwards and stood with one hand on Pa's

shoulder and the other on Ma's to brace myself. "As fast as ever," I answered.

"Did you bring the pound entry fee?" Ma asked.

I checked for the hundredth time. "Yes, Ma'am. It's right here in my pocket." As soon as we arrived, I leaped from the wagon and entered Lady in the race.

Pa and I hadn't practiced with the hessian bag this year because I was much too busy, and too worried, getting Lady ready for the horserace. Frank and his father won first place; Pa and I came in second. Mr. Carson was angry with Mike for some reason, so he raced with Jimmy instead. They came in last.

I watched the brumby-roping contest without really seeing it. I was worrying about the two mile race. How was I going to turn Lady around the rock at the end of the first mile? Ernie had been right: Lady was hard to turn. When she ran at full speed, it was impossible to slow her down for a turn. I had to run my race differently. But how?

Leaving the brumby-roping early, I worked my way through the crowd to be with Lady. Frank followed me.

"Mike's planning something," he said. "I heard Jimmy talking with someone in the dunny."

Alarmed, I asked, "What's he going to do?"

"I don't know. I'll try to keep an eye on him. He bet money that you'll finish last."

I looked around for Mike. "Where'd he get real money?" I asked.

"Probably stole it from his father."

"Thanks for telling me. I'll keep my eyes open."

"See you later. And good luck!" Frank disappeared into the crowd.

Pa arrived as I rubbed Lady's legs to get them warm. "It's time for the race, Casey. You'd better get saddled."

I hurried to our wagon for the saddle and blanket. "Pa! Someone's cut the cinch. What am I going to do?"

"There's no time to repair it. Go to the judge and get your entry fee back."

"You mean quit the race?" I couldn't believe that Pa thought I should pull out.

"I don't see any other choice," Pa answered.

"Well, I do!" I grabbed Lady's reins and leaped onto her bareback. Feeling my excitement, Lady spun around in circles. She was ready to run.

"You'll never stay mounted under full gallop!" Pa said.

"I'll manage!"

Five minutes later, twenty horses were nervously pacing back and forth near the starting line. Ernie reined his horse to a halt beside me. "Casey! Why you riding bareback?"

"Someone cut my cinch."

"One of the kids bullying you?"

"I think so, but I can't be sure."

"Well, good luck. I only wish I weren't riding against you. I've got to do my best to win."

"That's the way it should be, Ernie." I glanced at Ernie's horse. It was a long-legged sorrel. "Though if you hear Lady and me breathing down your neck near the finish line, move over a little to let us by," I said, grinning.

Ernie laughed and leaned over to shake my hand. "That's the spirit. Good luck."

The judge beat the butt of his pistol on the podium. "Will all the riders – I say – will all the riders please calm your horses and get in some sort of line. Spectators, please clear the raceway." He waited a few seconds before continuing. "Now, you all know the course. It's two miles, straight down for a mile, around the large boulder with a red flag on top, and back to the finish line, right here. There'll be no pushing and shoving. This is going to be a fair race."

The news of my bet with Mr. Parkes must have traveled from station to station, because every family who could possibly be at the rodeo was now gathered near the starting line. As the judge raised his pistol, the crowd became quiet.

"Riders, take your marks!"

I looked down the long straight-of-way and concentrated on the race ahead. Lady tensed beneath me.

The gun fired. A roar went up from the crowd as the horses pounded out of the picnic area. Lady started in the middle of the pack, then fell back.

"Come on, Lady, stretch it out! Don't let these old nags outrun you!" I felt Lady gathering momentum as her strides became longer. Before we reached the turning rock, Lady had passed the slower horses. All three of Mr. Parkes' racehorses were still in front. The problem of turning Lady around the red flag now confronted me. Should I stay close to the rock and swing wide on the final leg, or should I swing wide before I reached the boulder? I decided to swing wide before I reached the turning point. I glanced over my right shoulder to make sure the way was clear and reined Lady out wide under full gallop.

I was a hundred feet wide of the pack when I started my swing around the red flag. The fastest horses were slowing to make their turn as I leaned over for Lady to turn. She wouldn't!

"Lady, turn! You've got to turn!" I yanked the reins harder than I had ever yanked before, forcing Lady's head sideways. She did her best to turn without slowing down.

I grabbed her mane with one hand and leaned into the high-speed turn around the boulder. It looked as if we were on a direct collision course with the rest of the horses. Lady had no intention of slowing down to let any horse in front of her. Me, Lady and the pack disappeared behind the rock at the same time. Lady whipped around the rock. Somehow, she managed to cross in front of the other racers as they slowed for the turn. She kept her balance and maintained her speed. And, somehow, I managed to stay mounted.

We were now directly on the heels of Mr. Parkes' three racehorses for the final run to the finish line. The horse Ernie was riding looked as if it would be impossible to catch. Lady easily caught up to the first two horses. For a short time, we raced side by side while Ernie was still twenty feet in front.

I turned the reins loose and leaned forwards. Lady felt my weight shift and must've heard me talking in between her gigantic strides. "Go, Lady, go, Lady, go, Lady, go!"

Lady stretched and lowered her belly close to the ground as she pulled away from the two horses and closed the gap with Ernie. The finish line was rapidly approaching. I was almost crying with frustration.

"Lady, Moonrunner will be killed! Come on, girl. You've got to win! Moonrunner saved your life! Please, girl. You've got to save his!"

Ernie glanced over his shoulder and saw me running beside him. He grinned. It was going to be a close race. I barely heard the noise from the crowd's yelling as we raced between the two long lines of people. We both were doing everything possible to make our horses go faster. Lady was matching the racehorse stride for stride. We crossed the finish line as one.

I heard the crowd yelling "Casey won!" as they swarmed around us.

I found Ma and Pa in the crowd. I slid down from Lady's back and held her reins, waiting.

"The judge is takin' his time," said Pa. "He knows the story about you and Moonrunner. And he knows the crowd wants Mr. Parkes to lose because he has such a bad temper. And nobody likes a consistent winner."

Ma said, "Look – the other riders didn't have a chance to cross the finish line because of the crowd."

We all waited impatiently. Ma said, "Casey, stop walking in circles."

The more the judge hesitated, the more I worried. As he conferred with the rodeo committee, I started walking in circles again. This time, Ma didn't stop me. She had her hands together, praying.

I heard someone say, "Omeo has never seen a wilder race. What a finish!"

After fifteen minutes, the judge approached Ernie and me and handed each of us ten pounds. "It's a tie. You were exactly even at the finish."

I looked at the money in my hand and felt my stomach tighten. I didn't know what to say. I hadn't lost Lady but I hadn't saved Moonrunner. My deal with Mr. Parkes was that I had to win the race. We hadn't said anything about a tie.

Mr. Parkes settled it when he approached through the sullen crowd and took the money from Ernie. "Too bad, Casey. You ran a good race. You can keep Lady, but you didn't win Moonrunner. Ernie, I'll see you back at the station." Then he shook my hand and walked off.

Ernie turned to me. "I'm sorry, Casey. I wish I could do something. We finished in a dead tie. That must mean something – good friends like us shouldn't go around beating each other."

I looked down at my unpolished boots. I had failed Moonrunner. "When do you think Mr. Parkes will spirit-break Moonrunner?"

"In a few days, I imagine. He's a man of action."

I kicked a rock angrily, skinning my boot. "What will Moonrunner be worth when he's half dead?"

"Not much," Ernie answered. "Five pounds at the most."

"Do you think Mr. Parkes will take ten pounds for him now?"

Pa put his hand on my shoulder and said, "Son, you're going to need that money. If Lady's going to have a foal, she'll need extra food and vet care."

"Pa, what use is it if Moonrunner is killed and I don't feel like riding anymore? I made a promise to Moonrunner. There's something between him and me, Pa. We have to help each other."

"Why don't you go ask Mr. Parkes?" Pa said.

The crowd followed as I approached Mr. Parkes' buggy. I waited for them to fall quiet before I spoke.

"Sir, can I speak with you a moment?"

"No, Casey. You can't work for the black stallion and earn him like you did Lady."

"That isn't what I wanted to talk about." I paused. The ten pounds felt hot in my hand.

"What is it, boy?"

Ernie said, "He wants to buy the stallion with his winnings."

"He's worth more than ten pounds. Ernie, you said yourself you've never seen a more powerful, more spirited horse."

I answered quickly. "He'll only be worth five pounds if his spirit is gone."

The pressure of the crowd must've made Mr. Parkes feel uncomfortable. "Look, Casey, that may be true, but there's no guarantee his spirit will be broken, is there?"

"There's no guarantee he'll live through being broken!" I answered. "Then you'll have a dead horse on your hands and probably feel pretty bad about killing him."

"Casey! That's enough." Ma said sternly. "You mustn't talk to Mr. Parkes like that. You should always be polite – even when he isn't!"

Mr. Parkes sighed loudly. "What are you going to do with the stallion if I sell him to you?"

"Turn him loose."

The crowd remained silent as they waited for Mr. Parkes to speak. I looked directly into Mr. Parkes' eyes. He stared down at me and I refused to back away. I had made my offer.

It was several moments before Mr. Parkes finally spoke. He slowly extended his hand. "Give me your money, Casey. You can pick up the stallion at the station."

The crowd went wild, cheering, whooping and hollering. They picked me up and carried me on their shoulders around the buckjumping yard. I had saved Moonrunner!

★ CHAPTER SIXTEEN ★

Taming Moonrunner

I took my usual seat on the tailgate of the bullockwagon on our way home with Moonrunner.

We'd dropped Lady at the house before traveling on to Mr. Parkes' station to pick up the black stallion. Moonrunner was limping.

"They sure treated him rough, didn't they Pa?"

"Sure did, son."

"Think he'll recover?"

"He'll be all right. Ernie had a good look at him. He's just bruised."

"When will we get home?" I asked.

"We'll be there when we get there," Ma answered.

"Looks like his leg is bothering him more, don't you think?"

"He'll be fine, son," Pa said. But I was still worried. Every time Moonrunner limped, my heart tightened.

When we got home, I tried to give Moonrunner some hay and water, but he refused to take anything.

After supper, Pa said, "By the way, Casey, you ran a good race today. Ridin' bareback! Real smart how you managed to go around that boulder."

"Oh, yeah. I almost forgot all that happened today."

"Did you ever find out who slashed the cinch?" Ma asked.

"I think it was Mike Carson. Frank told me that Mike was planning something. He bet real money that I'd finish last."

"I was very impressed with the way you behaved today," Ma said. "You're a real gentleman, Casey Jenner. And your English is really improving. I'm proud of you. Now, you'd best get to bed."

With drooping eyes, I answered, "Thanks, Ma, for everything. I don't know why I'm so tired."

I went into my room. I wanted to sleep, but my mind was racing. After a few minutes, I burst back out into the sitting room. "Pa, I don't want to free Moonrunner until he's well and can take care of himself. Moonrunner must be strong enough to fight for some more mares."

"Okay, Casey. That's what we'll do. Now, get to bed."

"How can I get him to eat?" I asked. I slouched against my bedroom door.

"Here's what you must do. Keep Lady and Lop Ears in

the shed, away from Moonrunner. I'll stake Bossie up near the spring. In the mornin', carry a bucket of water to the yard. If Moonrunner doesn't drink while you're standin' there, take the water away. The important thing is not to leave water in the yard. He has to know that you're his only source of water and food. Tomorrow night, do the same thing again. Sooner or later, he'll have to drink."

"How long will it take?"

"Most horses, it takes only a few days. It might take longer with Moonrunner. If my guess is right, he had nothing to drink at Mr. Parkes' station."

I returned to my bedroom and shut the door, but I still couldn't sleep. From my bedroom window, I watched the shiny black stallion limping around the corral in the moonlight, restless in his desire to be free.

As I lay in bed, I heard Pa say, "It's nice what you said to Casey."

"There's a good man inside that boy that's just starting to shine," Ma said. "He's growing up so quickly."

"He's still a boy, but he faces his problems like a man. A lot of men I know face problems like they were still boys. But I'll bet if you made somethin' special for him, he'd eat it like a boy."

Ma laughed and said, "I'll bet he would. And I'll do that very thing." I smiled in the dark.

———✦———

The smell of breakfast cooking woke me the next morning. I leaped out of bed and bolted out the front door before Ma could stop me for breakfast. I was wearing the same clothes I had worn the day before. I didn't remember falling asleep, but I remembered Moonrunner. I quickly filled a bucket with water and entered the yard.

Pa was beside the shed, standing as still as a statue so he wouldn't frighten the stallion.

"How's he doing?" I asked, without taking my eyes off Moonrunner.

"Not so good. He's still limping," Pa answered. I offered Moonrunner the water, but he still wouldn't drink.

"Maybe by tonight," said Pa. "Let's have breakfast."

"I'll give Lady some exercise after."

"That's a good idea," Pa answered.

Moonrunner didn't eat or drink that night or the following morning. "Pa, if this keeps up, Moonrunner will die right here and I'll be no better than Mr. Parkes."

"He's a long way from dyin', son. Moonrunner has a strong will, which includes a will to survive. I've been watchin' from the shed. He's weakenin'. Did you see his ears flick this mornin' when he saw you? And he moved his head up and down as if he was tryin' to walk to the water bucket but his feet refused to budge."

That evening, Moonrunner slowly crossed the yard towards me. He took a quick gulp from the bucket at my feet and leaped backwards. I remained motionless as I quietly talked to him. The stallion approached the bucket again, keeping his eyes on me. He quickly emptied the bucket with loud sucking gulps.

"Good boy. See? That didn't hurt, now, did it?"

Moonrunner trotted to the far side of the yard. I left the yard and returned with a pitchfork full of fresh hay. "Want something to eat, Moonrunner?" But the stallion didn't approach the hay.

Taming Moonrunner was easy from that moment. Although he refused to drink the next morning, Moonrunner gladly drank from my bucket that evening after standing in the sun all day.

Several days later, Frank, Maggie, Mary and little Gracie came to see the black stallion. He was eating and drinking out of my hand. They watched from the hayloft as I entered the yard and set the bucket of oats at his feet. When Moonrunner nosed the bucket, I moved slowly to the stallion's side and petted him. At first, Moonrunner jumped away from my touch. But I persisted. Once he'd decided that I wasn't going to hurt him he let me stroke his back while he finished eating. I returned to the shed with the empty bucket, smiling.

"When are you going to ride him?" Frank asked.

"There'd be no sense trying to ride Moonrunner. Lady's the only horse I'll ever need." Lady must've heard her name because she stuck her head through the shed window and nickered at me, wanting her share of the oats.

Gracie asked, "Can I feed Moonrunner?"

"He's afraid of everyone except me. But you can give Hoppy an apple." The kangaroo had just entered the shed. I waited for Gracie to climb down the ladder and handed her an apple from Lady's barrel. She gave it to Hoppy and laughed, her brown eyes sparkling with delight.

Frank said, "After the way Mr. Parkes treated Moonrunner, I'm surprised he doesn't trample you."

"He's a friend," I answered. "Friends have to trust each other, even during the bad times. Things'll get better when I turn him loose."

"You're really going to turn him loose?" Mary asked.

"Sure. That's why I bought him. If something happens to our crop of hay, Moonrunner must be able to take care of Lady again this winter. He can't do that penned up."

"What if someone else traps him?" Gracie asked.

"Don't worry, Gracie. Everyone in Omeo saw me buy Moonrunner from Mr. Parkes, so he'll always be mine, whether he's running free or not. The high plains cattle aren't fenced in, are they? Everybody knows who they belong to."

"They're branded every spring," Frank said. "That's how they separate them."

"There's no other horse like Moonrunner in this area. That's brand enough."

Maggie said, "You ought to keep him for next year's race. It's the short one. I'll bet Moonrunner could beat any of Mr. Parkes' horses."

"I thought about it," I said. "But I don't believe

Moonrunner could ever get used to a crowd of people. No telling what he'd do. Besides, Moonrunner is a free spirit. Knowing he is out there, running free, makes me feel good inside."

We spent another hour at the yard watching Moonrunner and talking. Then we decided to ride up to my hideout to look for black cockatoos, loaded up with sandwiches from Ma.

———•–•———

By the first of May, Moonrunner was whinnying loudly at sunrise every morning for me to get out of bed and feed him. His health and his spirit had returned. It was a beautiful autumn morning. Dropping hay on the ground at his feet, I petted his neck and rubbed my hand along his withers. He no longer flinched when I touched him. I leaned against his side just to see what he would do. He merely braced himself against my weight and kept eating. Stepping on the gate, I gently leaned over Moonrunner and carefully placed all my weight on his back. When the stallion didn't jump away, I twisted slowly around and sat astride his back.

Moonrunner took a deep breath as if he was going to throw me. He looked around. Slowly, he released the air from his lungs and continued eating. I could have put a rope on the stallion and ridden him around the world at that moment. I was ecstatic! I sat quietly on Moonrunner's back for a long time and stroked his neck. After a time, I slipped gently down, picked up the empty feed bucket and headed for the shed. Pa was smiling.

"It's time, Pa," I said.

"Figured it was. I saw you on his back. Why don't you try ridin' him?"

"Can't do that. I told him he'd never have a rope around his neck again, except when I lead him back to the hidden gorge."

"Why did you get on his back?"

"I just wanted him to know that all men aren't bad. Now that he knows, it's time to turn him loose. Winter's coming."

"When do you want to free him?"

"It's a fine day. Might as well do it now," I said. "I'll saddle up and take him out to where we trapped Lady."

"Mind if I ride along?" Pa asked. "And I'll bring your ma."

"Be glad to have the company," I answered.

Pa saddled Girlie and Lady while I put a rope around Moonrunner's neck. As I led the stallion from the yard, I said, "I know this old rope doesn't feel good, Moonrunner. It'll be the last time. You're going to be free again."

It was an easy ride to the hidden gorge. Ma and Pa rode Girlie behind me as I led Moonrunner towards the Mitta Mitta River. I turned up the familiar trail and, stopping at the spring, pulled Moonrunner beside me and untied the rope. Moonrunner just stood there looking at me.

"Well, take off. Get going. You're free." I reined Lady down the gorge for home. Moonrunner followed close behind. "You don't understand, Moonrunner. You're free. Go on!" The stallion wouldn't leave Lady's side.

"Slap him on the flank," Pa said.

"Can't do that. But I've got an idea." I reined Lady in a tight circle and galloped up the gorge at breakneck speed. Moonrunner ran beside us, stretching muscles he hadn't stretched for a long time. He was soon in front, leading Lady through the bushes.

When we reached the old trap, I suddenly reined Lady to a halt while Moonrunner kept running. His tail flowed behind him and his black mane floated in the wind as he tore up the side of the canyon. He didn't stop until he reached the top of the spur. For the first time, he realized where he was and the old feeling of being a horse in the wild must've surged through his veins. He looked down at me sitting on Lady's back, standing in the middle of the old trap. He whinnied loudly – a long, piercing whinny. Then he whirled and disappeared beyond the rim of the gorge.

I yelled, "Goodbye, Moonrunner! You're free! You belong to this wild country, not to me, not to anyone. You made me understand this wild country. I love you, Moonrunner." My voice echoed off the gorge walls. I already felt lonely, missing one of the best friends I'd ever have. There was no other way to describe my feelings for Moonrunner.

Pa led the way home. Ma had her arms around Pa's waist. None of us spoke as our horses picked their way along the trail. I was happy for Moonrunner and proud of myself for helping a friend. It felt great doing something and expecting nothing in return. I tingled with happiness. I knew that I now belonged to this wild country and would always feel as free as Moonrunner was in the hidden gorge.

⋆ CHAPTER SEVENTEEN ⋆

The Last Blizzard

By the first of June winter grass had begun to sprout around the homestead. Unlike last year, I knew Lady had to winter with the brumbies because we didn't have enough hay. And it was nursing Moonrunner back to health that had caused the problem. The stallion had eaten all of Lady's winter provisions. But this year I was confident that Moonrunner would take extra good care of Lady for me. After all, we were friends. There was a bond between us that no one could ever break. I didn't complain this year about having to feed the work animals first. I had learned my lesson the hard way: first Old Lop Ears had saved me from the blizzard and then Girlie had rushed me to the doctor in Omeo.

So when Pa and I set out with Lady to find Moonrunner,

I knew we were doing the right thing.

───── ◆ ─────

We were camped beside the spring in the hidden gorge. It
had been a frustrating two days of fruitless searching.

"I wonder where Moonrunner's hiding," I said.

"My guess is farther north," Pa said. "Away from the river.
There's two traps in his old stompin' grounds. He'll never
come this way again."

"Lady and me found some pretty rough country up
there," I said. I was chewing on a piece of jerky. "I know one
thing, it's getting cold."

"Did you find a big gorge with a large round boulder in the
middle, near a spring? I discovered it last fall when I was hunting."

"I must've missed it," I answered. "You think Moonrunner
could be there?"

"Can't say. He sure ain't here."

"Can we reach it before dark?"

"If we ride hard," Pa said. "It's quite a piece down the
Mitta Mitta."

We reached the large gorge at dusk and camped near
a spring, where we discovered fresh horse tracks. The next
morning, Pa said, "Let's try farther north. They've got to be
here, somewhere."

I looked around. "It's a nice gorge for Moonrunner. I
wish we could've been here last night. I think he was standing
on this very spot."

"I'll bet you're right. Those large tracks look like his."

By mid-afternoon we'd searched five smaller gorges along the Mitta Mitta River. At the top of a sharp, narrow spur, Pa reined Girlie to a halt and leaned forwards in the saddle. "What do you think, son? You 'bout had enough of woolly butts and snow gums?"

"Lady's getting awfully skittish. Moonrunner must be close by. Let's turn her loose and see what happens."

"Won't hurt to try," Pa answered. "For sure, she can't do any worse than we have." We rearranged the pack so I could ride Old Lop Ears. I turned Lady loose.

"Look at her go! She smells something!" I yelled. I jumped onto the mule's back and trotted clumsily after Pa's faster horse. "Don't lose sight of her!" I shouted, doing my best to keep up, but it was futile. Girlie, Pa and Lady disappeared in the brush ahead. I was left behind, kicking the mule's sides to make him go faster. Feeling pretty useless, I rounded a large bush and slammed straight into Girlie. Pa was sitting quietly in the saddle, looking over the rim of the gorge. I turned Lop Ears so I could see and followed Pa's gaze to the bottom of the gorge. Five brumbies were below. Lady was standing on a knoll with Moonrunner. The black stallion and Lady were looking up the trail in our direction.

"He's wondering if you're here," Pa said. "See if you can coax him with a few oats."

I dismounted and grabbed a small bag from the pack. As I hurried down the trail, I ripped opened the bag, talking as I ran.

"Hello, Moonrunner. Remember me? I got some oats here for you, boy, got some oats."

Moonrunner stood motionless until I was halfway down the trail. He alerted his mares to the danger by nickering several times. They stopped eating and circled behind him for protection. The stallion trotted part way up the trail. We stared at each other. There was an invisible barrier keeping us apart.

"I know, boy, this is your kingdom. You're free now. You don't need my help. But listen, old friend, I need your help. I need you to take care of Lady for me again. Can you do that for old Case?"

I placed the open sack on the trail and backed away. "I understand, Moonrunner. Some other time, huh? We'll save it for some other time." When I reached Pa, I said, "He recognized me but was too proud to eat from my hands. He no longer needs me."

"That's true, son. But I'm sure he won't forget you. He knows where to come if he needs help." Pa backed Girlie away from the edge. "We'd best get gone. It's a long ride home. Old Lop Ears ain't as fast as Lady. We don't want Ma to burn the rabbit stew."

Pa turned up the trail along the edge of the Mitta Mitta while I stood for a long time facing Moonrunner. We gazed at each other, privately communicating thoughts. Eventually I decided it was time to leave. I wasn't around to see Moonrunner trot up the trail, but I heard his muffled nicker as he smelled my scent in the air and buried his nose in the oat bag.

<hr>

It looked as if we were going to have an early spring. Warm weather with no snow! Each day, I grew more excited about bringing Lady and her new foal home. Pa felt the winter was going to have one more say before spring truly arrived, but I couldn't wait another week. I decided to get Lady myself.

Without telling my parents, one beautiful morning, instead of crossing the bridge and going to school, I turned Old Lop Ears down the creek. The mule managed to cross the Mitta Mitta without any problems and continued plodding down the river trail. At the mule's slow pace, I reckoned we'd reach the large gorge by dark. Much too slow! All I had to eat was my school lunch, so I wanted to be home by dinnertime. I kicked Lop Ear's sides with my heels.

"Come on, you dang-burned mule! Giddup!"

The blue sky had turned light grey within a few hours. Then it quickly turned dark grey, then black. I reined Lop Ears into the large gorge. The temperature had plummeted from cool spring to freezing winter. I buttoned my sheepskin coat and reined the mule to a stop. Pa had been right. Winter wasn't through with us yet.

It only took a second to realize that I had to get home. As I turned the mule around, heavy snow started falling, blown in my face by a nasty wind. I couldn't see the mule's ears in front of me. I'd seen enough snow in Montana to know that this was going to be a bad storm. I'd never make it home through the blizzard. I had to find shelter. I remembered that the cave Frank and I had discovered was nearby. The cave was big enough for Frank and me to stand in, but not big enough for a mule. I reined Lop Ears up a small canyon, out of the wind, and slid down. I removed the saddle and saddle blanket, tied the reins so the mule wouldn't step on them, and slapped him on the flank. "Get home, Lop Ears! And this time, don't wait for me." The mule quickly disappeared in the storm.

I spent the next few hours gathering firewood. After the last time I was caught out, I had carried matches with me all the time. The howling wind felt like it was from the South Pole itself. Eventually it was too dark to gather more wood. I barely made it back to the cave dragging a dead tree branch.

The storm raged. Each time the wind dropped I rushed to the opening of the cave to see if it was over, but the storm intensified into a full blizzard.

I was warm inside my cave. I sat on top of my sheepskin coat and got a great fire going. Around dinnertime, I ate my school lunch and thought of Ma and Pa sitting around the warm fire. They would be worried because I hadn't arrived home from school. But I'd be home for breakfast. All I had to do was make it through the night. Old Lop Ears would bring Pa here by morning.

The storm raged all night. In the morning, I stacked more

wood on the fire to keep it burning. I slowly sucked on the two lumps of sugar I had brought to give Lady.

All day and all night the wind howled across the mouth of the cave. I was hungry and starting to worry about Lop Ears. Maybe the mule hadn't made it home. Maybe Old Lop Ears had drowned in the Mitta Mitta River. That must have been why Pa hadn't arrived to save me. Tears welled in my eyes. I loved that old mule. I drank melted snow and slept, dreaming of chocolate cake. My wood was running low. The cave was getting colder and colder.

After my second night in the cave, I woke early, shivering, clutching my sheepskin coat. My fire was out. The wood was totally gone. Why hadn't Pa found me? I ran around inside the dark cave, jumping, waving my arms, trying to keep warm. I bumped my head and fell hard on my back. Rolling over, I thought, *Wouldn't it be funny if Pa didn't find me until summer? A frozen corpse, that's all he'd find. A frozen corpse with a red bandana around its frozen neck. I don't want to die, Pa! I'm too young!*

I felt dizzy. I searched my pockets and found two matches. Saved! I lit one and looked for wood. I smelled flesh burning, but never felt the pain as it became dark again. *One match left. Don't waste your last match! Wood. That's it. I must find wood. Where's Pa?*

I suddenly felt hot. I rubbed my neck furiously. *My red bandana! I'm still wearing my bandana! That's why Pa hasn't found me.* I couldn't stop giggling at my own stupidity. *Of course! That's why he's not here. I didn't tie my red bandana to a tree to let him know where to look.*

Still giggling hysterically, I untied the bandana and crawled to the opening of the cave. Snow, so much snow! I clamped the bandana in my teeth and crawled out of the cave. *Sunshine! The storm's over! Find a tree. Tie bandana to tree. All white. Snow drifts. Dizzy. Blackness all around. Must think. No tree! No tree! I'll be a tree. I'll sit here. Wait for Pa. He'll see the bandana. Don't need a tree! Pa always comes. I'm cold. Pa? Pa?*

———◆·◆———

My body tingled with heat. Too much heat!

"Lop Ears! Lop Ears, I'm sorry!"

"Lop Ears is fine, son."

Ma's voice reached into the blizzard and pulled me out.

"Lop Ears … the storm …"

"Lop Ears is safe. He's in the shed. You're home," Ma said.

"What happened?" I opened my eyes. Ma was sitting beside me, holding my hand. I looked around. "How'd I get here?"

"When you didn't come home in the snowstorm, we figured you'd spent the night at school. Pa saddled Girlie and rode over there. Miss Evans was alone. She'd sent everyone home when the storm started. She told us that you'd never arrived at school. Then we knew you'd gone searching for Lady and were caught in the storm. Miss Evans, bless her heart, got in her buggy in the snowstorm and rounded up all

200

the neighbors. We've all been searching for you for three days. Frank and his father, Maggie and Mary and their fathers, and the Carsons. They all spent the night here during the storm."

"The Carsons? Were Mike and Jimmy looking for me?"

Ma nodded. "It was Mike who found you near the cave. You were stiff with cold."

I was having a hard time focusing. "Are you sure Lop Ears is safe?"

I realized Pa had been standing nearby all the time. "He's in the shed," he said. "I've just fed him."

"I've really been trouble, haven't I?"

Pa said, "You just decided to do somethin' right at the wrong time. How ya feelin'?"

"I'm hot," I said.

"Are you hungry?" Ma asked.

"I don't know. Is there any food left?"

Ma laughed. "Rabbit stew. That's about all. The cupboards are empty. I think there's a piece of cornbread in the oven."

———•◆•———

It was a few days before I was strong enough to go back to school. When I entered the classroom, the kids stood and cheered. Embarrassed by the attention, I quickly sat down and opened my book bag. I was thankful when Miss Evans started her lesson for the morning.

During recess, I found Mike and Jimmy standing near the

dunny looking lost. I crunched across the frozen white snow in their direction. There was no wind. The sky was deep blue, a perfect day. It was hard to believe how things had changed.

As I approached, I said, "Thanks for finding me, Mike. I wouldn't have survived without your help."

"You're welcome, Casey. When I saw you sitting in the snow with that red rag in your mouth, I fired my rifle to tell the others. It was our signal. Your hair and eyebrows were all white."

"Ma says you worked harder than anyone trying to find me ... Why? I thought you hated my guts."

"I had a long talk with Miss Evans during the storm. She said I was acting just like my father. I don't want to be like him so I figured I should make up for what I'd done to you."

"Friends?" I asked. I stuck out my hand.

Mike took it, grinning broadly. "Friends," he said. As we turned for the schoolhouse, he said, "I've got something I've been meaning to ask you, Casey. What's the real reason you canceled the bet after you won the race to the Anderson place?"

"I didn't want you touching my horse," I answered.

Mike laughed. "Can't blame you." After another long silence, he said, "I'm sorry I burned your baseball bat."

"I would've broken it over your heads, anyway."

"Yeah, I know."

I shrugged, "It burned pretty good."

"Must have been the American wood," Mike laughed.

I said, "If you ever want to get away for a while, just

come over to my place. No one needs to know. We can just sit in the hayloft and say nothing if that's what you want."

A ray of hope sparkled in Mike's eyes. "Thanks," he said. "I just might do that. I really do hate my father!"

There was another long silence. Mike popped his knuckles nervously. "My Pa was really angry when he learned I burned your bat. But it was just another excuse to beat me. I got three whippings and he made me go to bed without dinner and wash the dishes for a week. I couldn't see out of my left eye for a long time." Mike stuffed his hands into his pockets. He asked, "Want to go riding after school?"

"I'd like that," I answered. We walked towards the schoolhouse. Jimmy followed.

"What about your chores?" Mike asked.

I grinned. "They can wait."

Maggie and Frank were sitting on the school steps. She asked, "Did you find Lady?"

I shrugged. "The storm hit so suddenly I didn't have time to look."

"When are you going out again?" Frank asked.

"As soon as the snow melts."

"I'd like to come along," Maggie said.

"Me, too," Frank said.

"Count me in," said Mike.

"Me, too," added Jimmy.

★ CHAPTER EIGHTEEN ★

I Find Lady

I did my best to wait. I watched the snow slowly melt each day on the way to school riding Lop Ears. Each morning when I rode across the bridge, the call to turn north grew stronger and stronger. One morning, I saddled the mule and left for school, but turned down the creek as soon as I was out of sight of the house. My heart had won the battle. I thought about riding to school and getting my friends, but decided it would take too much time. Besides, Lady was my horse. Moonrunner was my friend. It was up to me to find them.

The river was half full of melted snow as we waded across. It was the nicest day so far that spring. The old mule was acting young again. I reached the big gorge by noon and sat down on a warm rock to eat my school lunch. Young, green shoots of grass could just be seen peeking their heads through the damp ground. But there wasn't enough grass near the spring to feed hungry brumbies.

"Looks like Moonrunner took them in search of food," I said to the mule. "Let's follow their tracks out of the gorge. What do you say, Lop Ears?" I reined the mule towards the Mitta Mitta. "Tracks go both ways. Now what?" I came to a halt. "At least they didn't cross the river. Since we didn't see them before, they must be further north."

In the next gorge, Lop Ears slowed his pace to a crawl. I tried to make the stubborn mule go faster, but it was futile. And it was just as well, because I was suddenly surrounded by brumbies. If I had crashed through the brush, the wild horses would have bolted and disappeared. Moonrunner was standing in front of his mares with his ears pointed in my direction. He sniffed the air and watched me approach. My heart was racing.

"Hello, Moonrunner. I see you made the winter. You look terrible! You're all shaggy and skinny. It must've really been tough."

I slowly circled the brumbies. There were three mares, each with a small foal standing by its side. The foals hid shyly behind their mothers with only their awkward, skinny legs showing beneath. I guessed they were less than a month old. I looked for Lady and her new foal as I moved around the mares. Completing the circle, I reined to a halt and looked at Moonrunner. "Lady's not here." The black stallion nickered at me. "Where's Lady, Moonrunner? Take me to Lady."

The stallion whinnied loudly and charged past me. The mares with their foals followed. The brumbies disappeared in the brush. I heard the stallion whinny again. "He wants us to follow. Come on, mule! Giddup!"

Old Lop Ears set his own pace down the bushy gully behind the brumbies. No amount of kicking from me could make the mule go faster and no amount of brush could make him slow down. I leaned over the saddle and hung on as bush after bush tried to knock me loose. I followed the fresh tracks along the river. While I was studying the tracks, the black stallion whinnied again. Moonrunner had turned into the big gorge with the spring.

"What's he trying to say?" I said aloud. I was excited about seeing Lady again. "Is Lady hurt? I reckon she needs me. Wish Pa was here!" I bounced on the mule's back as he trotted up the gorge. "We're coming, Lady, hang on! This dang-burned mule just won't go." Brush scratched my face and bare arms, but I didn't feel anything.

"Where are you, Moonrunner?" I whistled softly and the stallion answered. When I rounded the boulder near the spring, the black stallion was standing in the shadows near a snowdrift. He pawed the ground and snorted wildly.

"What is it, Moonrunner? I don't see Lady. There's nothing here. Stop playing games. Where's Lady?"

Moonrunner stopped pawing the ground and used his nose to throw snow from the snowdrift. He looked at me and nickered again.

"What are you trying to tell me? Is the spring under the snow and you want me to uncover it? Be glad to – then we'll find Lady." I slid down from the tall mule and approached Moonrunner. The brumby backed away. I dug in the snow with my hands. Instead of finding water, my hand hit something stiff and furry. I brushed a little more snow away and uncovered the reddish-brown hide of a dead horse. Now I had both hands madly flying, frantically tearing at the snow. I recognized the white blaze on the horse's face, but I kept digging until all four white stockings were uncovered and there could be no doubt. Lady was dead. She had died in the blizzard.

I screamed at Moonrunner. "You did it! You were supposed to take care of her. We had a bargain. I hate you! Get out of here! You're not my friend anymore." With tear-filled eyes, I charged the stallion and frightened the mares out of the gorge. Moonrunner galloped away.

I returned to Lady. Looking down at her, I muttered, "It wasn't Moonrunner's fault. It was me that killed you, girl. I couldn't feed you." I slumped to the ground, waiting for tears that wouldn't flow. Everything I had ever wanted was now gone. I felt empty. Moisture drained from my throat and left my voice raspy.

"I'm sorry, girl. I tried to find you sooner, honest. It was the blizzard, Lady. The blizzard stopped me. Please understand: I tried to find you."

I removed Lady's saddle blanket from Old Lop Ears and

placed it over my dead mare. When the tears finally arrived, I fell on the blanket and cried. I was too exhausted to move. Everything was over! Everything was gone.

I slept until dark and awoke to find absolute silence around me. Moonrunner had not returned. The gorge held a loud quietness as I looked around, trying to remember where I was. I was cold and hungry and all alone. I built a fire beside Lady and sat up most of the night remembering the fun I had had with her. I drifted in and out of sleep and had strange, disturbing dreams.

Daylight found me waking beside smoldering embers. I was too stiff and sore from the cold to stand. For another hour, I tried to decide whether it'd be easier to go home to face my parent's pity or run away. Since I had no supplies or money, I had to go home. The sun finally eased over the rim of the gorge and warmed my chilled bones. Old Lop Ears was waiting patiently, as only a mule can, still tied where I had left him the day before.

I piled brush on top of Lady. "I don't want buzzards eating you, girl." Before covering her completely, I lingered a moment with my hand on her neck, where she loved to be petted. "Goodbye, Lady. You were the best and the fastest horse in the territory. I'll miss you, girl." Tears rolled down my cheeks. I quickly threw on the last of the brush and ran for the mule. "Let's get out of here!"

Old Lop Ears trotted down the canyon and turned south towards the homestead without changing his neck-rattling speed. I heard a horse galloping behind me and reined the mule to a stop. I looked around. It was Moonrunner, running without his mares.

"I'm sorry. I just can't help you now. Our bargain is over!" I turned for home again. The stallion followed. I stopped again. "It's finished. Go on!" I tried to kick Lop Ears into a gallop. It was a wasted effort, because the mule had never galloped in his life. Moonrunner followed, sticking with me no matter which way I turned. I finally dismounted. The stallion approached and stood quietly in front of me. I knew then what Moonrunner was doing. He was offering to replace Lady: to be my horse. He was being my friend while I was being hateful.

Tears leaped into my eyes again. "It won't work, boy. I don't ever want another horse." Moonrunner didn't seem to be listening. I shouted, "Why can't you understand! I don't want you to be my horse!" I slapped Moonrunner hard on the flank. "Go on, get out of here!" The stallion ran a few feet and stopped. I mounted Lop Ears and turned back towards the Mitta Mitta. Moonrunner followed. Spotting his mares grazing in the new grass along the river, I stopped the mule and pointed. "There's where you belong, Moonrunner, with your mares. You wouldn't like being a station horse, penned up all day." My voice became gentle. "Now, go. They need you more than I do. You've got to be free."

Moonrunner ran towards his mares, stopped halfway and looked back at me. Then he disappeared around the nose of the spur, running like the wind to the north.

"Goodbye, Moonrunner. Thanks for staying true." I turned for home, knowing I'd never ride this way again.

★ CHAPTER NINETEEN ★

Moonrunner Returns

Life was over for me. With Lady gone, all I wanted to do was crawl away somewhere and die. Why should I have the privilege of living when she was dead? I yearned for school to be over so I wouldn't have to face my friends' questions and pitying eyes. I hid food and clothing beneath my bed in preparation for running away. I'd get to Melbourne and catch a ship back to America. The tears I hid from my parents flowed openly in the darkness of my bedroom. I stood for hours in front of my window looking at Lady's empty yard.

One night, Pa saw me standing at the window as he returned from the shed. "Can't sleep?"

"No, sir. Not for a few nights now."

"It won't do any good pinin' for Lady."

"I can't forget her that easily, Pa. What kind of friend would do a thing like that?"

"Do you think she'd want you to starve and wreck your health with no sleep?"

I was silent for a moment. I said, "Please, Pa, I want to be alone."

"Your ma and me want to get you another horse."

"So it can die like Lady? I don't want another horse!"

"Casey, nothin's ever the same. It's always changin', hopefully for the better, but sometimes for the worse. Your ma and me have really been makin' a go of this place, thanks to your grandpa. We've had bad times and good ones. When it was bad, we almost gave up, but somehow, we hung on a little longer. Eventually things changed. I'm not askin' you to forget Lady, just accept the fact that she's gone. That's all. If I could bring her back, I would. Nobody can do that."

"Getting Lady and now ... now ..." I fought the tears back, but they squeezed from my eyes.

"Let's go into town in the mornin' and find another horse. You can't expect Old Lop Ears to carry you around the countryside and do the plowin', too."

"I'd rather walk, Pa. Besides, I'm staying home for a while."

"Okay, son. We'll do it your way. You've always been a dreamer, full of curiosity. Don't give up! Don't stop dreamin'. I wish that I was more like you, sometimes. I just wanted you to know that." He turned to leave, then paused. "At least try to eat a little more, just to please your ma. You know how womenfolk are, always worrying."

I smiled weakly, "Yeah, I know."

It was two weeks before I finally consented to looking
for another riding horse. But my heart wasn't in the search.
I spent all morning at the livery stable in Omeo riding every
horse that was for sale. Nothing pleased me. The horse would
have a short neck, or its gait would be broken, or I just didn't
like the color. We returned to the homestead in time for
supper without buying a horse.

The spring planting kept me too busy for feeling
miserable. By the beginning of summer, when the plants were
growing and doing well and the school year was nearly over
and there was nothing to do around the homestead, I felt
lost. Memories of exploring with Lady last summer filled my
thoughts from dawn until long after dark. I was dreading the
summer holiday.

I was slipping back into my depression when
Moonrunner suddenly appeared, standing alone on the ridge
overlooking the homestead.

Pa saw him first. "Isn't that Moonrunner?"

I was plowing weeds at the time. I dropped the leads to
the mule and left the plow stuck in the ground to keep Lop
Ears from drifting back to the feed bin. "It sure is. I wonder
why he came back. Do you think he needs help?"

"Probably just wants to pay you a visit. It's been almost
three months since you last saw each other."

I walked to the edge of the field and looked up at the

black stallion. Moonrunner reared high in the air and ran halfway down the slope towards me. He stopped as abruptly as he had started and stood motionless, waiting for me to do something.

"I think he wants you to go up and say hello. Take him some oats."

"It's awfully mean of him to come here now and bring back all the memories, Pa."

"I reckon it's a good thing. Stay in the open so he can see you. I'll get the oats." He quickly came back and handed me the bucket. I didn't make a move. Pa said, "Well, you goin' or not? Seems like if someone came all this way to see me, I'd at least have the courtesy to walk across this little field and say hello."

I looked at Pa for a moment and nodded. "You're right, Pa." I walked slowly across the field. The old excitement of seeing Moonrunner stirred in my veins. My pace quickened. Soon, I was running with the bucket swinging wildly in my hand. When I had nearly reached him, Moonrunner spun and disappeared over the ridge. I stopped running and yelled, "Don't leave, Moonrunner! I've got some oats for you. I'm not mad anymore. Please come back." The stallion had disappeared.

Hanging my head, I turned for the house. The bucket of oats slapped against my leg as I plodded down the slope. I heard Pa shout, "Moonrunner's returned!"

This time he wasn't alone. The stallion pushed a little foal down the hill towards me. When Moonrunner and the foal reached the foot of the hill, the three of us stood together. The black stallion ate the oats as I made friends with the foal, speaking softly to her.

As soon as he finished eating, Moonrunner wheeled and trotted up the hill. His drab winter hair was totally gone, leaving behind a shiny new coat. His mane and tail were like silk blowing in the wind. Suddenly, Moonrunner stopped, looked down at me, gave a loud whinny and broke into a full gallop towards the Mitta Mitta River. I held onto the little filly until Moonrunner was out of sight.

I knelt beside the filly for a few minutes to calm her, petting her neck, then struggled to lift her in my arms. She was too heavy. I pulled her across the field towards the house. She fought every step of the way. Ma and Pa ran out to help. With Pa on one side and Ma on the other, we gently led the filly into Lady's old yard. She continued to buck and kick wildly around the strange enclosure.

"He brought me a filly, Pa. Can you believe it? A little filly." I was jumping with excitement.

"A beautiful little thing, isn't she?" Ma said.

"Did you notice she looks just like Lady? She even has a blazed face and four white stockings."

"I noticed," Pa answered, smiling.

"How old you think she is?" I asked.

"She looks about three or four months."

"Then she could be Lady's," I said.

"It's possible. If she was born before Lady died, another mare could have raised her," Pa answered.

"Does that happen?" Ma asked.

"If the other mare has lost her foal."

"Gee," I said. "Lady's filly. I just know she's Lady's. That's why Moonrunner brought her down."

"She was probably too young to travel when you found Lady. Moonrunner waited until she could be weaned, and made you a present."

"Lady's little filly," I repeated.

"It's a lot of work raising a foal, son," Pa said.

"I won't mind, Pa." I suddenly felt good again. "Why don't we go into Omeo in the morning and get me a riding horse for my birthday? It's coming up, you know. I've a feeling I'm going to need a horse this summer to keep my eye on Moonrunner and make sure no one traps him. After all, we still have a bargain, him and me. And besides, Moonrunner will want to see how well I'm taking care of Lady's filly."

Ma asked, "Have you thought about a name?"

"I thought of one, but ..." I hesitated, my hand still resting on the gate.

"Are you going to call her Lady?" Ma asked.

"No. There'll never be another horse like Lady. I thought I'd call her Little Lady. Do you think Lady would mind?"

Ma was happily crying. "I don't think so, son. I don't think so."

I latched the gate and paused as I looked back at Little

Lady standing in the morning sun. She whinnied weakly to me. I swelled with pride. I was already daydreaming about the summer ahead.